Return to Me
© by Erin O'Reilly 2015

Affinity E-Book Press NZ LTD
Canterbury, New Zealand

1st Edition

ISBN: 978-1-927328-93-4

Editor: Nat Burns
Proof Editor: Alexis Smith
Cover Design: Irish Dragon Designs

Acknowledgments

Thank you Affinity eBook Press for once again having enough faith in my story to publish it. As with all my stories I get to work with an exceptional group of women who encourage, cajole, and at times breath fire to help me write the very best book I can. Julie, thank you for being my confidant at those times when I just couldn't get the words out. Nanc, thanks for the beta read and the great cover. Thanks also goes to Terry, Lisa, and Sandy for reading Return to Me and giving it the green light for publishing. Last, but not least, thank you Nat for the editing and Alexis for the proof edit—you're both the best.

I would be remiss if I didn't thank everyone who reads my stories and lets me know what they think, either good or not so good. It all goes toward learning the craft of writing.

Return to Me

Erin O'Reilly

Return to Me

Erin O'Reilly

An Affinity Suspense Romance

Affinity
eBook Press
NZ
2015

Dedication

For Nanc (Irish Eyes)
A wonderful friend and a great sounding board.

Table of Contents

Also by Erin O'Reilly

If I Were a Boy
Through the Darkness
Deception
Fearless
'55 Ford
Fractured
Revelations
Wolf at the Door
Sandcastles

With JM Dragon
Earthbound
When Hell Meets Heaven Series
New Beginnings
Atonement

Prologue

Darkness filled the room and a moldy stench permeated the air. The cold from the hard, damp floor she was laying on infiltrated her body, making her shiver uncontrollably. She wanted to curl up into a tight ball to find some warmth, but her wrists and legs were bound. Thirst begged to be quenched and when she licked her lips, her tongue stuck to the dry, cracked skin. How long had she been there? Syd took an inventory of her body. She was naked and she could tell from the pain in her abdomen and on her face that she'd been beaten and the cold puddle she was lying in was, most likely, her own urine. The ache between her thighs made her realize that there was a strong possibility that she'd been raped but couldn't recall the event if it had happened.

"Help," she called out in a weak voice that barely reached her own ears. "God, please help me."

As if her prayers were answered, she heard a door moan as it opened and she turned her head in the direction of the sound. Blackness prevailed as the sound of hard soles on concrete came closer.

"Help me," she cried.

A swift kick to her rib cage made her groan in pain. "Why are you doing this to me? Just kill me and be done with it," she said in a voice that lacked strength.

"Tell us what we want to know."

Syd frowned. She knew that voice. It couldn't be. But she knew in her heart that it was. "Why are you doing this to me, Carly? You've worked by my side for six years…why?"

"You couldn't keep your mouth shut and just do your job, could you? We were ready for a major breakthrough that would have prevented diabetes but you wanted to pull the plug."

She kicked Syd again, only harder.

"It will do more harm than good and you know it. That anomaly can't be overlooked." Syd's mouth was dry and it was painful to form words but she persevered. She needed Carly to understand and stop this madness. Syd closed her eyes and a vision of Ellie floated before her. *Oh, my love, I'm so sorry,* she thought.

"Kill me," she whispered. With her bound feet she kicked out, hoping to make contact—but met only air.

"Any success?" a male voice asked.

Where did he come from? Her head was killing her suddenly but she closed her eyes and searched her memory. The man had always been there.

"No, and I don't see that changing," Carly's voice answered.

"Then we have no choice. Sedate her, clean her up, and bring her to the operating room."

A needle pierced her skin.

Darkness.

Chapter One

The sun's early evening rays pierced the low, thin cirrus clouds and beat down on the narrow strip of sand that the incoming tide was gobbling up. Two women ran hand in hand along the beach, laughing as incoming waves slapped their ankles. Finally reaching the narrow path that led up and away from the beach, the two women walked a hundred yards before sitting on a large flat rock.

Ellie Scott chuckled as she took off her soggy running shoes and poured out the ocean's water. "I didn't think we were going to make it," she said.

"Neither did I," Sydney Tanner said, breathlessly. "If our running is any indication, I think we should start jogging again.

"Do you think we'll see it?" Ellie asked, pointing toward the west and the setting sun.

Syd looked up at the sky, then the skyline. "Clear skies. I don't see how we can't."

Both women watched as the sun seemed to make its way below the horizon. Just as it was about to disappear, they saw a green flash.

Ellie grinned. "Our record is still intact," she said as she gazed into her lover's eyes before they kissed. For the past nine years, on the anniversary of the day they'd met, they would come to sit on this same flat rock and watch for the green flash that occurred just as the sun set.

"Let's take this home." Syd pulled away and a look of love filled her face.

†

"What's wrong?" Ellie asked, when they got to Syd's truck.

"Nothing."

"Please don't give me that, babe. You've had that perplexed look on your face for weeks now. What's going on?"

Syd took Ellie's hand and kissed it. "It's not another woman, if that's what you're thinking."

"That never crossed my mind." Ellie laughed nervously. "Is it work?"

For the past six years, Syd had worked as a microbiologist for a medical research company. The work was always exciting, for it was on the cutting edge of new disease cures. She had always looked forward to going to work but that had recently changed.

"Please tell me," Ellie pleaded.

Syd turned her head and stared out the front window before looking back at her wife.

"It's the tests I'm doing…but I can't really divulge much." She shook her head. "I know what I have to do and I'll sort it all out when I get to work."

"You are the most ethical person I know. No way will you let something get by you." Ellie said. "I'm proud of you for always doing the right thing."

"Thanks. Sometimes you need to flex your muscles so people will take you seriously." Syd bent her elbow and grinned. "And I have some pretty awesome muscles."

4

Ellie reached out and squeezed the taut arm. "That you do."

Syd twisted the key in the ignition and the truck roared to life. "I think a pizza and a beer with my best girl is calling me."

Syd set her jaw. There was more to the story—a lot more—but the nature of her job wouldn't allow her to divulge anything until she resolved the mess.

"Sounds good to me if there's a leisurely bath after."

Syd smiled then nodded. "Are you reading my mind?"

"Always." Ellie took Syd's hand and squeezed it.

†

Later, lying in bed, naked and sated, Ellie sighed. "I wish this day would never end."

"Me too. I think we need to work it out better so that our days off sync more often than once every other week." Syd pulled Ellie closer and kissed her blond hair.

"Maybe I'll see if I can work the hours you do." Ellie laughed at the absurdity of her words. "But somehow I don't think they will go for three in the morning till three in the afternoon. It is the emergency room though, so who knows."

Syd moved and kissed Ellie before caressing her cheek. "Let's not worry about that now," she purred. "I have something important to do."

"Really? Whatever could that be, Dr. Tanner?"

"Let me show you, Dr. Scott."

They had been married for nine years, together for ten, yet the passion they felt for one another had never waned. It was rooted in deep desire and a love that seemed to extend beyond time and space.

Syd ran her fingertips across Ellie's body, eliciting moans of pleasure. "You are so beautiful, my love." Her mouth greedily took Ellie's—the kiss was deep and sensual.

Their lovemaking this time was slow yet fervent, each taking time to lavish the other with all the love they had. Sated they held one another, whispering words of love until they fell into a restful sleep.

†

At five the next morning, Ellie leaned down and kissed Syd's lips. "When you get home from work tomorrow morning, wake me, okay?"

Syd drew in a deep breath, smelled the fresh, clean scent of Ellie, and smiled. "It will be my pleasure."

Ellie raised her eyebrows. "Your pleasure is what I'm aiming for." She gave her wife one last kiss before turning to go.

Syd watched as Ellie sashayed toward the door. "You know that I won't be able to go back to sleep now, don't you?"

"Good. I hope you will be turned on all day thinking about what I'll be doing to you tomorrow morning," Ellie said over her shoulder.

Sitting up in the bed, Syd let the sheet fall away, exposing her breasts. "Come back to bed," she purred.

"God, I wish I could. You look delicious all rumpled and needy." Ellie looked at her watch and shook her head. "You don't know how badly I want to do that but I'm going to be late."

Syd grinned and crooked her finger. "Be late."

Ellie rushed to the bed and pulled Syd to her before kissing her passionately. "That will have to hold you until you get home. I've really got to go."

"I know. Don't like it, but I understand. Let's hope the day flies by for both of us." Syd kissed Ellie. "I want you."

Ellie growled and stood. "You are a temptress and I will think of nothing else all day."

†

That afternoon around six, Ellie opened the door to their home, went in and kicked off her red clogs. Looking around the room, she frowned.

"I wish you were here," she whispered as she put her work bag on the nearest chair.

Her day had been long and filled with drama as well as trauma. The emergency room had bustled the entire day with one emergency after another. Usually the people who came to the emergency room used it as an outpatient clinic but there were nine genuinely urgent situations that day. The one that stuck with her was a twenty year old woman who had arrived near the end of Ellie's shift with massive injuries, very close to death. Ellie knew that the woman, on life support, didn't have long but she worked laboriously to keep her alive. Her goal— to keep the patient breathing until her family arrived.

Ellie had firsthand knowledge of the guilt and sorrow people felt when they couldn't say goodbye. A few years ago, her mother had been lingering on the edges of death but had rallied and was doing so much better. A patient Ellie was treating in the emergency room had taken a turn for the worse so she had left her mother for a short while, promising to return soon.

When she returned an hour later, her mother had passed and Ellie never got to say goodbye. Now it was her mission to do all she could to keep someone alive until his or her family arrived.

That night, the slightly overweight young woman had opened her eyes and cried out for her mother.

"She's on her way so hang in there, Susie," Ellie had whispered.

Then, to make matters worse, Doctor Michael Creighton entered the room, prepared to harvest the patient's organs., Ellie met him at the door. In a hushed tone she hissed at him. "You can't have her yet."

"Is the next of kin on their way?"

"Keep your voice down," Ellie ordered. "The parents are on their way. I want you to leave them alone until they can say goodbye. There's nothing worse than you hovering over them when they are grieving."

"You're too soft, Scott. She's going to die so why not use her organs so someone else can live?"

Ellie shoved the man, eyes flashing. "First of all, she isn't dead yet and there is a possibility that she'll recover."

Creighton's eyes raked across the patient. "Yeah, right. Just keep her alive until I get the signature."

"I don't have a problem with that," she said through gritted teeth. "My problem, Doctor, is *you* hanging around like a vulture. This girl and her loved ones deserve to have some time together. Then you can feed on her."

†

Now, alone in the empty house, Ellie did what she always did when she lost someone so young—she cried. The sound of her cell phone announcing a text message caused her to pull the instrument out of her bag. When she saw the message from Syd, she smiled.

Just want you to know I love you.

The message didn't surprise her for it was always the same. What did puzzle her was how Syd always knew when she entered their home—it was as if she had radar or something.

I love you back, Ellie wrote in reply. She would have to be satisfied with that until Syd arrived home in about eight hours.

After a meal of leftovers, Ellie took a shower, then slipped naked under the sheets. She pulled out her eBook reader and opened the latest novel by Dean Koontz and began reading. She knew she'd eventually fall asleep and she looked forward to feeling Syd's lips on hers, waking her.

Chapter Two

Ellie stretched and yawned when her alarm went off.

"Syd?" she said to the empty room. She looked at the covers she'd turned down the night before—they looked the same. Jumping out of bed naked, she hurried around looking for her wife—she wasn't there. When she checked her phone, there were no messages or calls.

After pressing the speed dial number for Syd, she waited for her *hello* but all she got was Syd's voice saying, *leave a message.* Racing to her desk, she sorted quickly through a pile of papers until she found the number Syd had given her for emergencies.

"Paradyme Research," a voice said when the ringing stopped.

"Hello, may I please speak with Dr. Tanner?"

"Just a moment," the voice said and Ellie felt her body relax.

The voice returned. "Hello? Dr. Tanner left the building at three-fifteen this morning."

Ellie felt her body react with a shiver that started in her head and continued down her body. "Does anyone there know where she went? She hasn't arrived home."

"Sorry, everyone on that shift is gone now."

"Thank you," Ellie muttered before pressing the phone off button.

Once Ellie put on her scrubs, she slipped her feet into the red clogs and picked up her bag, then hurried out of the house. She drove her SUV out of the garage and began tracing the route Syd took to and from work. Once she arrived at Paradyme, she drove slowly around the parking lot looking for Syd's truck—it wasn't there. It was then, as she sat in her car in the parking lot, that her body began to shake uncontrollably.

"Syd, where are you?" she whispered.

Ellie engaged the Bluetooth phone connection in her car. "Call hospital."

"Calling hospital."

"Hello, Traci, this is Elinor Scott, I've had a family emergency and won't be in today. Can you call whoever is on call and ask them to come in?"

"I'm sorry to hear that, Doctor Scott, is there anything I can do to help?"

"Not at this point, but thanks, Traci."

"Any idea how long you will be away?"

"No, I don't know." She rubbed her hand over her face. "I really don't have any idea since it just happened. I'll know more later today." Ellie ended the call and laid her head on the steering wheel trying to get control of the fear that swamped her.

When she raised her head, she reengaged the phone. "Call Jill."

Jill answered right away. "Hi, sis, shouldn't you be at work?"

"Jill," Ellie cried.

"Ellie, what's wrong?" Jill said with alarm in her voice.

"Syd...Syd is gone."

11

"Gone...like she left you?"

"No...she disappeared and I can't find her. I checked her work, the parking lot, and the route she takes. It's as though she disappeared off the face of the earth."

"Are you home?" Jill asked.

"No, I'm sitting in the parking lot at Syd's work. Her truck isn't here and they said she left at her usual time this morning."

"Ellie, go home and I'll meet you there. We will figure this out, okay?" She paused. "Are you okay to drive?"

"Yes, I'm fine. I'll see you at the house."

✝

Thirty minutes later, Jill opened the front door to her sister's house and found her on the couch with her arms wrapped around her legs as she let out anguished cries. Rushing to her sister, Jill pulled her close and rocked her.

"Have you called the police?" Jill asked softly.

Ellie's shaking voice said, "Yes, they said I had to wait twenty-four hours to file a missing person report."

"That's ridiculous. Did you call any of the people she worked with last night?"

With eyes narrowing, Ellie glared at her sister. "What do you think I am...an imbecile?"

Ellie saw Jill shrink away and instantly regretted her words. "I'm sorry. That was uncalled for. You're only trying to help. I don't know their phone numbers. Syd had all those numbers on her phone." She shook her head. "I don't even know most of their names."

Sobs shook her. "She's gone and I don't know what to do."

Jill pulled her sister closer and gently stroked her hair. "We'll find her."

"How, Jill? How can we find her?"

"Have you called her folks? Maybe she went there."

Ellie lifted her head. "No, I haven't. I'll call them now."

With a shake of her head, Ellie ended the call. "They don't know where she is. Her dad said she called last night around seven and she seemed fine to him." She expelled a breath. "They are on their way here. Craig said he knows people at the police department that can help."

"That's good news." Jill hugged her sister tighter. "We will find her, I know we will. Why don't I get you a cup of coffee? Have you eaten anything today?"

"No. Once I realized Syd was gone, I just left to find her."

"Then I'm going to get you coffee and something to munch on. You won't be any good to anyone if you let yourself get run down."

"Thanks." Ellie tried to smile but failed.

"I'll be right back." Jill hurried out of the room and returned a minute later with a mug of coffee. "I couldn't find anything quick to eat. Do you want me to make you some eggs or toast?"

Ellie shook her head. "Coffee is fine for now."

A knock sounded on the door.

Jill patted Ellie's leg. "I'll get it." She got up and went to the door to open it. When she saw the anguished looks on Syd's parents' faces, she closed her eyes. "Come on in. Ellie will be happy to see you."

Ellie's tears had begun to dry until she saw Syd's parents and they started anew. She stood and they all hugged. "What are we going to do?" she cried.

"Sit down, dear, and tell us everything," Anita, Syd's mother, said.

Ellie explained everything that happened from the time she left for work the morning before until she woke to find Syd not there that morning. "I don't know what to do," she reiterated.

Craig patted his daughter-in-law's shoulder. "I'll call my friend at the police station and see if he can start the ball rolling before the twenty-four hour rule goes into effect." He left the room for the kitchen.

"The one thing I am sure of, Ellie, is that my daughter loved you and she never would have just left willingly. We *will* find her."

Ellie put a trembling hand to her mouth. "What if she is out there somewhere hurt and there is no one to take care of her? I can't imagine how frightened she must be."

"We don't know that, sweetheart. Have faith," Anita said, hugging Ellie close.

"I just want her to be safe and come back to me."

Craig came back into the room.

"Did you have any luck?" Jill asked.

"Yes. I've spoken to my buddy and he is going to make some inquiries at Paradyme. He is fairly certain that they have surveillance cameras and he is hoping to look at them today."

"Thank you, Dad. At least we will have a starting point then," Ellie said.

"He said if they can see her leaving, there is a good chance that they can use other cameras around the city to track where she went." Craig let out a sigh. "It's a start."

"I know we will find her," Anita said. She buried her face in her hands and began to sob. "We have to find our little girl."

†

That afternoon, Ellie, Jill, and the Tanners visited the police station to report officially that Dr. Sydney Tanner was missing. Craig's friend, Captain Tom Barth, took them into a room that was used for interrogation.

"Did you bring a picture?" the captain asked.

"Yes." Craig slid a photograph across the table. "This was taken two weeks ago. Right, Ellie?"

Ellie nodded.

"Can you give me a physical description of her, Doctor?"

"Yes, she is five seven, a hundred and thirty-some odd pounds, she has long, black hair, and hazel eyes that change to blue when she wears that color." Ellie's lips were pursed as she worked her jaw. "She's beautiful."

"Do you have anything, Tom?" Craig asked.

"Paradyme let us look at their videos and we saw your daughter leave work and get into her truck and leave the parking lot. 2014 yellow Ford F150 right?"

Both Craig and Ellie nodded.

Ellie gasped. "Did you see where she went?"

"We are still going through all the footage but I can tell you she went south after she left the parking lot."

"South?" Ellie frowned. "We live north of Paradyme."

"Is it possible someone was in the truck waiting for her?" Craig asked.

The captain's lips narrowed. "The tape malfunctioned from two-fifteen to three in the morning. It is possible that someone broke into her truck then."

Craig narrowed his eyes. "How possible?"

"I don't know, Craig. We need to look at any video we have going south. The problem is that she headed out of town and we don't have that many cameras in that area."

"So that's it?" Ellie glared at the man. "Can't you do anything else?"

"I have patrol cars checking the route out of town. As you know, that covers a lot of ground that becomes desolate scrub after about a mile."

Ellie stood. "Come on, let's go drive that way ourselves. It's better than waiting around. I know Syd and she wouldn't have gone south unless she had no other choice."

"Let us do our job, Dr. Scott. You will only impede our investigation if you go out and try to find her yourself."

"I have to do something." Her eyes opened wide. "A few days ago she told me she was having issues at work. She told me she was going to sort it out the night she disappeared. Certainly you can question her co-workers about that."

Captain Barth scribbled on a note pad. "Did she say anything else? Can you give me any other details?"

Ellie shook her head. "No. She's always been secretive about her work. I didn't even know the names of her co-workers to call and ask them if they saw her leave."

"Okay, I'll look into that." The captain looked at everyone. "I will make this my top priority and make sure that we get it out to the press in hopes that if someone saw her, they will come forward."

Craig stood and held out his hand. "Thanks, Tom. You will be in touch right?"

"Yes, I have your number and Dr. Scott's. I'll make sure you are kept in the loop at all times. If you have any questions or think of anything else that will help, please don't hesitate to call me." He handed everyone his card before looking directly at Ellie. "We'll find her."

The renewed tears that were stinging the back of her eyes threatened to fall. All Ellie could do was nod before she quickly exited the room.

†

That night after Jill left, Ellie sat on her couch, gazing at the evening news but comprehending nothing. Then she heard it.

"Police are searching for renowned microbiologist, Dr. Sydney Tanner who went missing after leaving work early this morning."

A picture—the one they gave the police—flashed on the screen.

Ellie couldn't breathe for it was all so surreal. She knew the smile on Syd's face was for her. Ellie had taken the picture at a picnic they'd had with Syd's parents two weeks before. "We were so happy that day," she lamented aloud.

"Police are asking anyone who may have seen Dr. Tanner or her yellow F150 pickup truck, license plate GRAM STAIN 10, to call them immediately. In other local news…"

Ellie picked up the remote and replayed what was just on and then did it again. She frowned as she replayed the video again. "Where are you, Syd? Why can't I find you?" Her mind once again focused on the words the newscaster said. *Renowned.* "I knew she had accolades for her work but *renowned*? Why didn't I know that?"

From the start of their relationship, they'd agreed that work would stay at work when they came home. If it was something significant, they would discuss it, but for the most part their work lives were separate from their personal ones.

That fact alone made Syd's comments about work the day before all the more noteworthy. Ellie picked up her tablet and searched for Dr. Sydney Tanner, microbiologist. Instantly she saw a picture of Syd along with a bio listing her accomplishments. There was nothing that Ellie didn't know, but she had to admit that after reading the information, she could see why someone would refer to her as renowned. Was someone at Syd's work jealous of her endeavors and wanted to get her out of the way?

The ringing of the phone startled her. "Syd?" she said when she answered.

"No. Sorry, sis. I just wanted to let you know I am home and only a phone call away if you need me," Jill said.

"I just watched a news report about her disappearance." Ellie began to sob. "What am I going to do if I can't find her?"

"I should have never let you talk me into leaving. I'll be there shortly. You shouldn't be alone."

"There's nothing for you to do, Jill. Stay home with your family. I'm fine."

"Like hell you are. I'm coming there, so get ready to answer the door."

"Jill…."

"Not working. If nothing else, I can be a shoulder to cry on and a sounding board. See you soon."

"But…" There was no sense in saying more—Jill had already hung up. Ellie let out a sigh. She was glad that she wouldn't be alone.

.

Chapter Three

The investigation into Syd's disappearance garnered a large presence on the local television stations and newspapers. Volunteers from the community rallied around the family, offering to search for Syd. Surveillance cameras picked up Syd's yellow truck leaving town. No other vehicles passed that point for twenty-three minutes, ruling out anyone following her. The camera clearly showed only Syd in the front seat with what looked like a gun resting against her head from the back seat. The camera five miles farther down the road did not show Syd or her vehicle.

"This narrows our search down to either side of the road for that five mile stretch," Captain Barth told Ellie and Craig. "A search party is on its way to the area as we speak."

"That's where to search then," Ellie interrupted. "What about the gun that appeared to be against her head?"

"Our forensics team could not say definitively that it was a gun...it could be some anomaly."

"Bullshit! You know as well as I do that it was a gun, Captain," Ellie spat out. "She's got to be there and she has to be alive."

"We want the same thing, Doctor," Captain Barth said.

19

Ellie put her hands on her hips. "I want to join in the search."

The tall burly police captain shook his head. "Let us do our job, Doctor. That's a big area to search. If you only go five miles in each direction that's twenty-five square miles. We have no evidence yet pointing to where she pulled off the road or how far she went when she did. Our people are trained to find out where that is. Once we've established the where, we can arrange for a walking search of the area."

"Can't we search with a helicopter?" Craig asked. "There isn't a lot of ground cover in that area. It should be easy to spot a bright yellow truck."

"First we have to find the where, Craig."

"Once we find out where she left the road, I'll personally hire a helicopter to do a search. It will much faster than a ground search," Craig said.

"I can't let you do that. This is police business and you cannot be involved."

"The hell I can't! That's my daughter out there and she might be hurt and in need of attention. I will not sit idly by while you take your sweet time." Craig stood and shook his head. "I'll do what I need to so I can find my daughter."

"And so will I." Ellie followed her father-in-law from the room.

"Please give us a day," the captain pleaded.

Craig turned and looked at his friend. "If it were one of your kids would you just sit idly by or do something?"

"I get that but I cannot allow you to interfere with our investigation. Remember, you came to me."

Craig stopped and closed his eyes. "Seems I have no choice in the matter."

"That is where you are wrong. We all have choices and I know what mine is," Ellie said softly. She tugged on her father-in-law's shirt sleeve. "Let's get going and start our own search."

"Please, both of you, let us do our job."

"It's been two days and you don't seem to have any more information than you did on day one. We haven't received any ransom demands or any other contact." Craig sucked in a breath. "I'm not stupid. I know that the longer it takes, the more the chance is that she's not alive. Right now we are wasting time. I know she's out there and needs us," he said. "I'm sorry if you don't like it, Tom—I have no other choice."

†

Once they were outside, Ellie turned to Craig. "Do you know where we can hire a helicopter?"

"We should wait a day, Ellie. Tom is right about us letting them do their job. Once they find out where she turned into the desert, we can get a helicopter."

"She might be dead by then. If she is out in that desolate place hurt she won't survive long. If that was a gun to her head then we haven't got a minute to waste."

Craig smiled fondly at Ellie. "You're right." He gave her a hug. "Let me make a phone call. I have a buddy who flies helicopters. I'll arrange for him to take us on a search of that area. After all, how hard can it be to spot a bright yellow vehicle from the air."

Ellie hugged Craig to her. "Thank you. We are running out of options."

"I know." Craig swiped at his eyes before pulling out his cell phone. "Let me make that call.

†

Ellie felt her stomach churning an hour later when she and Craig stood on the tarmac next to a blue and white helicopter.

"Craig, I'm sorry we have to meet under these circumstances," Ben, the pilot said, as he jumped out of the helicopter.

Craig took the man's hand. "Thank you for making the time to do this on such short notice."

"Glad to help out." Ben patted his friend's shoulder before turning to Ellie. "Ben Hildebrand at your service, Dr. Scott. From what Craig tells me we are looking for a yellow truck in a twenty-five square mile area just outside the city."

"Yes, that is right."

"It'll stick out like a sore thumb." Ben motioned to the helicopter. "Come on. Load up and let's take a look-see at what is out there."

Just as they reached cruising speed, Craig's phone rang. "It's Tom." He pressed a button. "Hello... Tell me where. We are in the helicopter now. The hell I won't. What if she is in the truck and needs help? I won't sit idly by. Okay, but if you aren't there within a few minutes, I will check myself. Will do."

"What did he say?" Ellie asked.

"Her truck turned right off the road after a mile and a half." Craig sighed. "He said not to land near the area and do not attempt to go there. We could compromise the scene by doing that."

"If we see the truck, I won't just sit here and wait. What if she needs medical help?" Ellie cried.

"He said that a team is in the area searching and if we find the truck, they will go right there." Craig took out a map and pointed to an area for Ben to see. "She is in this area."

"I'll have you there in ten minutes," Ben said above the roar of the rotors.

The ride in the helicopter was surreal to Ellie as she looked at the landscape below. She recognized the area to be near where Syd worked and her heart lurched as the thought of Syd alone and helpless without anyone to save her.

I told you I'd always be there for you. I'll save you, my love, if it's the last thing I do.

She saw two police cars making their way slowly along the ground below. "There are the police."

"Keep your eyes peeled for her truck," Craig said.

It didn't take long before Ellie gasped. "Look! There's her truck. It's in a ravine."

Craig took out his phone and called Tom. "We found the truck it is about a mile ahead of your cruisers. Okay... we will hover over the area until they get there. I won't, but once they get there, I'll have the pilot land and we will go and see for ourselves. I understand it's an investigation and we won't get in the way. Yes, I see them now so we are landing." Craig turned to Ben. "Can you land as close as you can without disturbing the area."

"Will do," Ben answered.

The helicopter landed and Ellie opened the door, jumped out and began running in the direction of the truck. She pushed through the scrub and the low trees that littered the area, intent on reaching the truck.

"Is she there?" she screamed out when she spied the truck.

A tall muscular man held out his hand. "Stay back! This is a crime scene and reporters are not allowed."

Ellie stopped dead in her tracks with her hand over her mouth. *A crime scene. Oh my God, she was dead.*

"No." She fell to her knees, ignoring the sharp pieces of shale that stabbed into her knees and legs.

"What did he say?" Craig crouched on the ground and cradled Ellie in his arms.

"A crime scene." Ellie struggled to get up. "I have to go see her."

Craig held her back. "Stay here. I'll go see what's happening."

"No," she said emphatically. "I'll go with you."

"Your legs." Craig pointed to the blood staining her trousers.

Ellie looked at her legs and frowned when she saw the blood but felt nothing. "It's unimportant…nothing else matters but finding Syd. I have to go to her."

Just then a police officer approached them. "You can't be here. Please leave the area at once."

Craig, still holding Ellie, stood, pulling her with him. "We will not leave. I am Syd's father and this is her wife."

"You still can't be here. It's an active crime scene," the officer reiterated.

Craig blanched at the officer's words. "Is she in the truck? Is my daughter dead?" he asked in a whisper.

"I cannot comment on that, sir."

"The hell you can't." Craig took out his phone and tapped in a number. "Tom, we are at the scene and…." He looked at the officer's nametag. "Officer McNally is giving us a hard time. All we want to know is if Syd is in the truck and what her condition is. Yes." He handed his phone to the officer. "Captain Barth wants to speak with you."

"Yes, sir. Yes, I understand. Will do, sir." The officer handed Craig back his phone. "If you will follow me, I'll take you to the scene."

Ellie grabbed her father-in-law's hand and put her other one over her mouth as her eyes scanned the area. Most of the people there were milling around, mainly looking at the ground, and she knew that if Syd was alive, there would be more activity around the truck.

"She's dead," Ellie whispered.

"Have faith."

"Dad, there's only one person by the truck and she isn't looking inside. That can mean only one thing." Ellie gulped back her tears.

"Or she's not there," Craig said softly.

"The truck is abandoned," the officer said. "We found some blood on the front seat and are now waiting for the crime scene team. Dr. Tanner's keys, wallet, and briefcase are in the vehicle."

Craig shook his head. "Did you see any footprints?"

"No. The wind has been heavy for the past few days and anything like footprints probably were blown away as soon as they were made. We were lucky to find the tire tracks. The captain said he'd be out here to speak with you shortly. If you will both wait by the helicopter, I'll let you know when he gets here."

It seemed like an eternity as they waited for the captain and for more information.

"What could have happened?" Ellie asked.

Craig shrugged. "Anything...I don't know. I just want my baby back."

"What will we do without her? She is my strength. My everything."

"Here comes Tom." Craig nodded toward the truck. "Hopefully, he will have more."

Tom Barth held out his hand and took his friend's hand in his. "Craig, I have some news."

"Where is she," Ellie asked.

"That we don't know, ma'am. We do know it is her truck. Her phone, keys, and wallet were all still there. There was a small amount of blood on the seat but the techies don't think it is a significant amount to warrant concern."

"What happened to her?" Craig asked.

Tom shook his head. "It looked like the truck just fell into that small ravine. Preliminary findings don't show any malfunctions it just looks like it rolled in and got lodged there."

"Were there any signs of a struggle?" Ellie asked. "Was someone else in the truck?"

"We won't know the answers to that until we get the truck back to the station and do a thorough investigation of the entire truck."

"So all you have is the truck," Ellie swiped at the tears threatening to spill onto her cheeks. "Syd is gone and you don't know if she is injured or where she is, do you?"

"No, not yet, but we aren't finished with our investigation. I've sent for Butch, our tracker dog, to see if he can find any scent to follow. We won't stop looking for her until we find her. I can promise you that."

"Thank you, Tom." Craig turned to Ellie. "Come on, let's go."

Ellie nodded at the police captain and climbed aboard the helicopter. Once the doors were closed Ellie touched the pilot's shoulder. "Do you think we can fly around the area and see if we can spot her?"

"We sure can. We have most of a tank and a lot of daylight left."

"How far do you think she could travel after the truck crashed?" Craig asked. "If she is injured and walks away, how far could she go in, say, two days?"

"Syd is strong and in good physical condition," Ellie said. "She's smart, too, so she wouldn't leave the truck until it was light and she probably went back the way she came. She might have made it to the road."

"What if she is injured? Would she be confused and go the other direction?" Ben asked.

"That's a possibility but I'd think if that was the case, she'd stay with the truck. She'd know I would come to find her."

"Then why don't I fly a grid that is four miles by five miles."

"Sounds good." Craig smiled. "Thanks, buddy."

†

The next day Craig and Ellie were back at the police station, sitting in Captain Barth's office.

"What can you tell us, Tom?"

"We've gone over the truck inside an out. Other than your daughter's finger prints, we didn't find evidence that anyone else was there."

"That's impossible," Ellie said. "I was in that truck the day she disappeared. You should have found my fingerprints on the passenger side."

"Maybe she had it detailed," the captain offered.

"When?"

"You said she was at home during the day. Maybe she had it done on her way to work."

"No way. I'm sure she had it detailed earlier this week." Ellie shook her head. "She wouldn't do it again. Syd had a standing appointment once a month for a detail." She fixed the captain with a glare. "What I am trying to have you understand is that *my* fingerprints should be in the truck."

"Did you look in her wallet to see if she had a receipt for a car wash on the day she disappeared?" Craig asked.

"Yes. We found none."

"What about the dog?"

Captain Barth looked away and sighed. "The dog tracked her scent back to the highway and east for about one hundred yards then lost the trail."

"Someone picked her up," Ellie said absently. "But she hasn't contacted us." She raised her hand to her mouth. "She's been kidnapped."

"Not necessarily. The crime scene folks found traces of blood on the steering wheel as well as on the seat."

"She could have a concussion and doesn't know who she is," Ellie said. "Or whoever has her is doing despicable things to her before they kill her."

"Now don't go jumping to conclusions. The story of Dr. Tanner's disappearance has gone national and that will give us a wider set of eyes looking for her."

Ellie looked away. Her world was continuing to crumble around her and her faith in the police finding Syd was waning. Syd was out there somewhere, floundering in a sea of darkness with no one to save her. "Bullshit. You know it and I know it, Captain. Just how far have we gotten in the past three days? All those eyes you talk about are useless."

"Don't discount the power of the media, Dr. Scott. They can be one of our most useful sources of information."

Ellie stood. "Pardon me if I don't agree with you, Captain. It's time I find myself an investigator who will find her…you obviously can't."

"Ellie, please. They are doing all they can. Let them do their job so they can find Syd." Craig looked at his friend. "I'm sorry. She isn't being herself."

"I don't need you to apologize for me, Dad. We all know that the longer this goes on, it will change from a search and rescue to a search and recovery. I can't sit by and wait for that to happen. Syd deserves better from me."

Ellie walked out of the Captain's office.

✝

Returning home from work, Ellie slouched on the couch. In every room, in every crevice in the house, Syd lingered. Everywhere she looked a memory of Syd filled her.

We were so happy. How did this happen? Return to me, Syd. Come home, this house is so empty without you here. Tears tumbled down her cheeks and she swiped at them, wondering if they'd ever stop.

The private detective that she'd hired had found no substantial leads after a month. In her heart she knew Syd was alive and somewhere out there, alone and afraid. She refused to believe that Syd was gone for good. Each day she'd drive the length of desolate highway where Syd's truck had been, searching for any sign of her wife. Family and friends who'd rallied around her didn't call or visit her anymore—obviously tired of her angst. So was she, but she couldn't give up. Giving up meant she had no hope and if that was the case, she might as well give up on life also. Yet, as her world continued to fall apart, she knew in her heart that she was giving up hope too.

Then Syd's parents suggested that they have a memorial service for their daughter.

"How can you do that? Syd's not dead…if she were I'd know it," Ellie had told them in a measured tone.

"Ellie, we need to do this so we can all move on," Craig said softly.

Looking at the man, Ellie saw the strain and sorrow in his face. His gray hair seemed to have turned white during the past month. His eyes, so much like his daughter's, were dull and lifeless. She reached out and took his hand. "As difficult as this is for me, I know it is doubly so for you and Anita. What can I do to help?"

Anita Tanner, a short round woman, whose horn-rimmed glasses were in her hands, shook her head. "You're supposed to outlive your children."

After she took some time then wiped her tears away, she spoke again. "I know how much happiness you brought to my daughter. Every time she said your name, her face would light up." She moved close to Ellie and put her arm around her waist. "That's how I know she didn't just disappear...she'd never do that to you or to us." The woman sucked in a deep breath. "She's gone and now it is time to have a proper church service for her."

All Ellie could do was nod. There was no way she'd give up on the hunt for Syd but she wasn't going to go against her wife's parents' wishes.

"What can I do to help?" she asked again.

†

Ellie stood expressionless next to the Tanners as people, many whom she knew, paid their respects. She couldn't bring herself to look at the large portrait of Syd that stood next to a large collage of pictures from her childhood. If she did, it meant she was buying into the notion that her wife was dead. She knew she wasn't.

Once the majority of people left the memorial service, her sister Jill approached. "You want to get out of here? I know I could use a drink."

Ellie's vacant eyes looked at Jill. "She's not gone. I'd know if she was."

Jill gathered her sister in her arms and pulled her close. "She will be alive as long as you remember her and keep her in your heart."

"You're saying the same things I've said to my patients' families after their loved one passes. Why won't anyone listen to me?" Ellie started to cry softly into her sister's shoulder.

"You'll get through this, Ellie. I promise you it will get better."

"How can you say that? I haven't seen her in a month...no one has. The case has gone cold." Ellie balled her fingers into a fist. "No one is looking for her anymore." She motioned to the room. "It's come to this. A sad goodbye to the one person who knows me better than anyone else. I need her strength to get through each day, Jill. That is why I cling to her memory and the knowledge that she will return."

Jill hooked her elbow into her sister's arm. "Come on. I'm getting you out of here. It's too depressing."

Gratefully, Ellie let Jill take her away from the memorial service. It was too much for her to bear.

†

Three months later, Syd was still missing and a new police detective, Jordan Laverty, was in charge of the case. Ellie called daily only to be told that the detective wasn't available. Deciding she was being stonewalled, Ellie went to the police department to confront the woman face to face,

Laverty was at her desk

"Detective."

The well-built woman with long brown hair pulled back in a ponytail looked up.

"Dr. Scott, why are you here?" she asked.

Ellie sat in a chair opposite the woman and gritted her teeth. "I want to know what you are doing to find Syd."

"I work on Dr. Tanner's case every day." Her hazel eyes held sympathy. "I search for women who are found lost and those that are found with amnesia. Every case I come across, I hope to see Syd's face but so far I haven't."

"I can't believe that after all this time you haven't found one shred of new evidence that would help you find her, Detective."

"Look, Dr. Scott, I've looked at the file numerous times and it's all the same. There's nothing in the truck or around the truck that indicated foul play. I wish I could have better news for you but I don't." She reached in her inbox and pulled out a stack of folders. "These are all the missing persons files I am working on."

"You've given up then?" Ellie frowned angrily.

"Look," she said softening her voice. "The case is still open but until we get more information there is nothing I can do. It's not like I can pull her out of thin air. I think you should consider that she may have intentionally disappeared."

"That isn't who Syd is. She didn't leave me…she'd never do that. Did you consider that maybe someone has taken her because she's a lesbian? Maybe some pervert picked her up on the highway and has her imprisoned." Ellie sucked in a breath. "There's always news reports about finding women who escaped from their captors. Have you looked into that?"

"I assure you, Dr. Scott, that we have investigated all those possibilities and some you haven't even considered."

"Like what?"

"Human trafficking."

Ellie's hand went to her mouth and her eyes flared wider. "Oh, my God, no," Ellie whispered.

"I'm not saying that is what happened, I'm only letting you know there are multiple reasons for a person to disappear. Unfortunately, all we have after all these months is that she left work around three-fifteen on the morning of April twentieth and we found her truck abandoned in the scrubland outside of town. There were no signs of a struggle in or around the vehicle."

"What about her blood on the steering wheel and the seat? What about the fact that no other finger prints were in the truck? I was in that truck the day before. My fingerprints should have been there."

The woman leveled her gaze at Ellie and shrugged. "I understand that there are discrepancies about the fingerprints but we have no leads. Yes, it seems suspicious. I wish I had more for you, but I don't."

"There has to be more," Ellie cried.

"We can't manufacture evidence," Jordan Laverty said again, in a gentler tone.

"So that's it?"

"What do you mean?"

"You've stopped looking for her?"

"As I said, the case is still open and I check on Dr. Tanner every day. We will keep looking for clues but you need to understand that from where I'm sitting, it looks like either she or someone else doesn't want her to be found."

"Did you check out her work again? She told me something was going on there."

Detective Laverty blew out an exaggerated breath. "There's nothing nefarious going on there. I went back and looked at the security footage and saw nothing untoward. I've interviewed her fellow workers and the administration and there is nothing that raises a red flag."

"Syd didn't just imagine there was something that she needed to fix. She's not like that."

"Look, Doctor, I've got work to do. If we find anything more, I'll call you."

Ellie stood and pointed a finger at the woman. "It's your job to find Sydney Tanner. She should be your number one priority."

The detective's phone rang. "I'll be in touch," she said before she picked it up.

Closing her eyes in resignation, Ellie got up and left.

Chapter Four

"I'll be out of town for a few days," Ellie told her sister when she entered the house. "Will you come by and check on things?"

"Of course I will. Where are you going?" Jill asked.

"I have a job interview."

"A job interview? I don't understand. I thought you loved your job."

Ellie bowed her head and shook it. "It's been months since she disappeared. I thought I could stay here and just go on but the memories are too strong. I need to see if I can find solace elsewhere."

Jill pulled her sister into her arms. "I'm here," she whispered. "Let me in. Let me help you get through this."

"Don't you see that I'll never get *through this*. Syd was my world—my everything. No matter where I go in the house, she is there. I can smell her, feel her, and at times I can almost reach out and touch her." Ellie buried her head farther into Jill's shoulder. "I think I'm going mad. I miss her so much that I wonder if I can go on."

"Is that why you want to move?"

"I don't know what else to do, sis. My world has collapsed around me and I'm trapped. I can't go back and I can't go forward. Maybe changing jobs and where I live will help."

"Are you going to sell the house."

Ellie pulled back and looked at her sister. "Are you crazy? When Syd comes back I don't want her to find strangers in our house? I'm keeping the house and leaving it just as it is."

"But you won't be here. How will she feel about that?"

"I'll leave a letter for her telling her where I am and to call me."

Jill shook her head. "Are you sure this is what you want to do?"

"Yes." Ellie began to sob. "It is either move away or commit myself to a psych ward."

After a moment, she shook her head and laughed through her tears. "That's rich. If I get this job that is exactly where I'll be working."

"Tell me about the job you are interviewing for."

"When I saw the name of the place I knew I was destined to apply for the job of medical director." Ellie shrugged. "It called to me and somehow I knew it was the right thing to do. I've not gone all clairvoyant, promise."

"What is the name of the place and how far away is it?"

"Salvation. It's about two hours southeast of here."

Jill's forehead wrinkled. "Medical director? You're an ER doctor, not a desk jockey."

"You forget, little sis, that I have a degree in hospital administration. From what I understand, I'd monitor the physicians and staff to make sure they're doing their jobs. I'm hoping to also have interaction with the patients, to make sure their needs are being met."

"You'll be like the boss *and* an advocate?"

"Yep. I'm sure about the admin part but will have to find out if I have any contact with patients when I meet with Salvation's current administrator." She shrugged. "I'll know more after the interview."

"When are you leaving?"

"Tomorrow morning. The interview is at three so I'll leave here around noon. That will give me plenty of time to get there. I've booked a hotel room for tomorrow night, then I'll come back the next day."

Ellie saw the worried look on Jill's face and pulled her into a hug. "This is for the best."

"I know but if you get the job and move away, I'll miss you so much...so will the kids."

"I haven't got the job yet and if I do, it's not like I'll be across the country. I plan on coming home often so I can be here when Syd comes back."

"If you are so sure Syd will be back, then why are you leaving?" Jill asked, watching her sister speculatively.

"I just need a change of scenery and if you think about it, I'm not really leaving, I'm just working elsewhere. I'll be here every weekend."

"I guess two hours away isn't all that bad, but still...." Jill seemed worried if Ellie left she would spiral downward into an abyss of further depression.

Ellie held up her hand. "Please don't say anything more. I am going to see about the job that's all. Nothing is firm yet, so please stop worrying. I haven't even had the interview, so until I know more, I can't make any decisions. It just feels right though, a gut instinct."

†

Ellie pulled up in front of the large, century old building that looked like money. There was no doubt in her mind that the people who stayed there were very well off. She continued on to the visitors' parking lot and for fifteen minutes sat in her vehicle trying to convince herself that she should go in. For the entire trip there her mind had carried on a running argument about the wisdom of interviewing for a new job. Her heart wasn't in it but something was telling her that it was the right thing to do. She wanted to turn around and go back to the home she'd shared with Syd and wait for her return. She felt like she had been set adrift on the ocean without a compass or direction.

"Because Syd is my compass," she whispered. "Help me, Syd. What should I do?"

Ellie buried her face in her hands. She was losing hope and the betrayal of Syd stabbed at her heart as her world crumbled even more. Her prayers went unanswered and she was falling into the darkness she didn't think she could ever climb out of or survive. A picture of Syd laughing suddenly appeared and Ellie trembled—Syd deserved better. Moving her hands she looked up at the deep blue sky through the sunroof and could feel the warmth and peace of Syd surround her.

"Please forgive me, my love, for doubting and losing faith in you. I won't dishonor you by letting my fears color everything. You will return. I know you will."

After pulling herself together by blowing her nose and wiping away tears, she sucked in a deep breath, pulled on the door handle, and got out of the car. It was time to move forward, knowing with certainty that Syd was not lost to her. Hope would always remain.

†

The atrium of Salvation's main building featured marble floors, wood accents, and a dome of stained glass. It was breathtaking in its lavishness. To the left, sitting behind a beautifully crafted antique mahogany desk, was a gray haired woman wearing glasses.

"Welcome," Madeline Spencer said. "May I help you?'

Ellie moved toward the woman. "Yes, I'm Elinor Scott and I have a three-fifteen appointment with Dr. Rojas."

Madeline smiled broadly. "Please have a seat there." She pointed to an antique divan that sat to the side of her desk. "I'll let Dr. Rojas know you are here."

Ellie nodded and moved toward the divan while the woman behind the desk picked up the phone.

The ambiance of her surroundings made Ellie feel at peace for the first time since she'd lost Syd. As she looked around the area, she tried to discern what exactly it was that made her feel that way. The air held a pleasant scent that she couldn't identify and the background music was so soft and soothing that if one wasn't listening they might have missed it. It certainly wasn't like any hospital she'd ever been in. Of course, Salvation wasn't an ordinary hospital. It was more of a retreat to calm and heal troubled minds rather than just injured bodies.

"Dr. Scott, how was your trip here?'

Ellie was shaken out of her contemplation and looked up. Assuming that the woman standing in front of her was Maya Rojas, the hospital administrator, Ellie stood and offered her hand. "Nice to meet you, Dr. Rojas. The drive here was uneventful."

"Did you have any trouble finding us out here in the middle of nowhere?"

Ellie shook her head. "Your directions were spot on." The hand that held hers was soft and warm and Ellie felt her body relax further. When she realized that the woman was

several inches taller than her she stole a look at her shoes—
no high heels.

"Five eleven," Dr. Rojas said grinning. "Too tall for
most dates but not tall enough to be a professional basketball
player.

With her cheeks burning, Ellie looked away. "I'm
sorry."

"Don't be, I get that a lot." The administrator touched
Ellie's arm and started walking. "Please join me in my office
and we can begin the interview."

Oddly, Ellie felt herself recoil from the touch and was
grateful that the woman didn't try to take her arm. "Okay,"
she said before walking toward the open door.

The administrator's office was like the atrium, warm
and inviting, and Ellie settled into a soft leather chair.
"Thank you for this opportunity, Dr. Rojas."

"Please call me Maya."

"Very well, Maya it is."

"I am very impressed with your résumé and think you
will fit in here nicely."

"What exactly does the position of medical director at
Salvation involve?"

"Basically, as the director, it would be your
responsibility for overseeing all aspects of the medical care
and the services we provide here at Salvation. As the medical
director you will provide leadership and evidence-based
management that promotes effective practitioner and facility
care processes and practices in several key areas...."

Ellie sat listening to Maya drone on about what the
job entailed and occasionally she'd ask questions but for the
most part she listened and digested information. The job
responsibilities were, in her opinion, doable and was
certainly less hectic than working in an emergency room.

The doctor was sitting directly opposite Ellie, allowing her to take in the woman's overall appearance.

Maya Rojas wasn't a beauty but was striking in appearance. Her face was angular in both her jawline and cheek bones but not so dramatic that it made her look gaunt. Jet black hair along with dark eyes that seemed to be smoldering only added to the allure of the face. Ellie shook her head and looked away when she heard the administrator speak.

"What do you think so far?" Maya asked.

"It all sounds very interesting. I do have a few questions."

"Please share."

"First, do you offer a 401K plan?"

"We have that. Next."

"Will I be on call during the weekends?"

"Hmm, not as a rule. Of course there will be times when we may need that if I'm unavailable."

Ellie nodded. "Good. I'd like to go back home on the weekends."

"Do you have family there?"

"Yes." Ellie had no intention of adding anything more. Her business was hers and not the administrator's. When she noticed that Maya was looking at her in what seemed anticipation of more, Ellie smiled. "Family is important to me."

"Yes. I believe it is to all of us. Especially here. The family members who visit the patients are invaluable to their recovery—unless it is a contentious relationship, then we discourage their visits."

"Do you have a lot of that?"

Maya shook her head. "More often than not family members want their loved ones to recover and leave here."

"What is the recidivism rate?"

"Quite low."

"How many long term patients are there?"

"Do you mean long term as in never leaving or being here longer than six months or a year?"

Ellie thought for a moment. "More toward never leaving."

"Very few." Maya tapped her fingers against her lips. "For the most part, all our patients are here to recover from too much stress in their lives, either from work related or alcohol and drug abuse problems."

"Okay, that clarifies the medical needs for me."

"Right," Maya said with a smile. "The salary for this position is one hundred seventy one thousand."

Ellie frowned. "That is considerably less than what I'm presently getting."

"Yes, I know, but we do have benefits to go with the position."

"Such as?"

"We have cottages on the property that are provided to certain staff at no cost. We pay for all the utilities along with providing cable and internet."

"A cottage as in a one room place with a bathroom."

"No. No, not at all. The one I am thinking of has three bedrooms, two baths, kitchen, living room, and a dining area."

"Garage?"

"No. But there is a carport."

Ellie calculated the cost to buy or rent a home in the area against the decrease in pay and frowned. "Still...I'm not sure it will be enough to offset the difference." She looked at the administrator and saw what she thought was disappointment in her eyes. "But, I would save in gas. I take it that this cottage is within walking distance."

Maya brightened. "Yes, it is. In addition, we have a state of the art gym that the staff can use."

"Do the patients have a separate facility?" Ellie asked. "Physical activity is a good way to help with addictions."

"There is a separate gym for the patients. About six months ago I instituted a policy that all our patients that are able must have physical activity at least twice a week."

"Is there a trainer for them?"

"Yes, we have a full time trainer."

"Nice. It sounds like you are proactive in patient care. I've seen many places where patients are strapped to chairs in front of a television."

"Not at Salvation," Maya said.

There was an awkward silence that seemed to stretch into minutes. Finally Maya stood and Ellie followed, taking the offered hand and shaking it.

"Thank you for the opportunity to interview for the position," Ellie said letting go of Maya's hand.

"Come. Let's take a short tour of Salvation so you can see for yourself what a fine facility it is."

"Okay." Ellie followed the woman out the door. Just as the atrium was soothing, so was the rest of the building. Everything seemed to be subdued and relaxing, incorporating a state of the art facility with peace and tranquility.

Once the tour was finished , Maya guided Ellie back to the atrium where she once again offered her hand.

"Thank you for coming, Dr. Scott. Right now, I imagine you need time to digest everything you've seen and heard. If you have any additional questions, please don't hesitate to call me. Otherwise, I'll be in touch later this week."

Ellie took the hand and shook it. "I'll look forward to hearing from you."

"Take care and be safe on your drive home."

Ellie nodded and turned for the door. After hearing the door close behind her, she practically ran for her car and once inside, locked the doors. She was shivering and a fine sheen of sweat covered her body. For more than an hour she'd held it together and now in the safety of her car her emotions took control.

"Oh, God, what am I doing here?" A quick look at her watch told her she had time to cancel her hotel for the night and still get home before eight. Once she'd cancelled her reservation, she headed for the safe home she'd shared with Syd.

†

Ellie saw Jill's car in her driveway when she got home. "Hi, I'm home," she called out, entering the house.

Jill came out of the bathroom with her hand over her heart. "I thought you were staying overnight."

"I changed my mind. I needed to come home."

Jill's brow creased. "Was the interview that bad?"

Ellie shook her head. "No. It was good."

"Then why the sudden urge to come back here?"

Ellie wrapped her arms around her waist protectively. "It was too good to be true." She shrugged. "I think I'll be offered the job and that terrified me."

"Why?"

"You still don't get it, do you." It wasn't a question. Ellie knew that no matter how she tried to express her feelings about Syd, no one would ever fully understand the deep rooted connection they had. "Because Syd won't be there with me," she whispered.

Jill moved forward and pulled Ellie close. "She's always with you."

"I know that, but at the moment that thought doesn't help."

"If you're offered the job, will you take it?"

"I don't know." Ellie longed to be alone so she could revisit all the memories of Syd that still lingered. "Thanks for taking care of things here. The upside of me coming home tonight is that you are off guard duty." She smiled and stepped back. "Go home and enjoy being with your family. Life is too short not to embrace every moment you have together." Ellie's voice, as always, held a tinge of sadness.

Jill snorted. "Guard duty indeed. You know, if you had a cat or a dog this place wouldn't be so quiet.

"I like the quiet." Ellie opened the door. "Text me when you get home, okay?"

"Sure thing." Jill kissed her sister and smiled. "I love you."

"I love you, too. I'll call you tomorrow."

When the door closed, Ellie let out a sigh of relief before she headed to the bedroom to crawl under the covers and dream of Syd.

Chapter Five

The woman known as Jane stood in front of a large window in the sanitarium and watched as rain pelted the glass. Her slender finger touched a raindrop and followed it as it coursed down the pane. She sighed deeply—she didn't know why, but rainy days made her feel pensive and sad.

An arm slid around her shoulders and Jane turned her head to see a round woman with a pleasant face smiling at her.

Marie Hendricks, the floor nurse, studied the patient and smiled. "Everyone is waiting for you. Tommy said he can't wait for the chance to beat you at Scrabble."

Jane reached up and patted the woman's hand. "Not today," she said before touching the scar on the side of her head that was hidden by her hair. "I need to go lay down. My head hurts."

The nurse tightened her grip on the patient's shoulder. "Do you want me to get Dr. Rojas?"

With a shrug, Jane moved away from the nurse. "No. I just need to sleep it off."

"Okay, but I'll check in on you later."

Jane smiled and moved toward the security of her room.

In her small room, Jane sat on her bed with her knees bent to her chest and rocked slowly. The pain searing through her brain was worse than ever. When she heard the door open, she did not look up—she knew who it was.

"I told Marie I didn't need you." She grimaced. "That's the last time I'll trust her to keep her word."

"She's worried about you, Jane, and so am I. We've discussed this—you need to let us know when the pain starts so we can treat it early."

"I don't want to live on drugs. I can handle the pain, so go away and let me do that."

"From the looks of you, I find that hard to believe." Maya Rojas said. She moved closer to the patient and put a comforting hand on her arm. "Lay down and I'll give you a shot to ease the pain."

Jane hurt too much not to comply. She lay down then rolled onto her side. When she felt the doctor pull down the waist of her sweatpants, she braced herself for the usual sting. Once the doctor moved away, Jane rolled onto her back as she felt the Dilaudid begin its journey through her body.

"Now, you'll feel better." the doctor said in a soft voice. She sat down on the edge of the bed. "I'll stay with you until the worst of it passes."

Jane began to feel the effects of the drug and closed her eyes before she yawned. As Maya turned to move away, Jane grabbed her wrist and pulled her back. "Don't you let them hurt me anymore," Jane begged as she twisted the doctor's wrist.

"Stop," Maya cried. "You're hurting me."

"I know that once you give me the shot he comes—the man with the white hair. I know what you let them do to me." Jane glared at the woman. "Don't let them come this time." A tear coursed down her cheek. "Please," she pleaded.

"Let go of my wrist." When the grip loosened and her hand fell to her side, the doctor leaned in and let the back of her fingers gently roam across Jane's cheek. "I won't let anything happen to you," she whispered.

The words were lost to Jane as the drug numbed her body and mind. When she heard voices, she tried to focus on the words but she couldn't—everything was a blur.

"Is she ready," a man's voice asked as he entered the room.

Maya turned and looked at the man who was dressed in black but with snow white hair. "She knows what you do."

"Impossible."

Shrugging, the doctor gave the man a serious look. "She just told me that she knows who you are."

The man placed a black case on the table next to the bed and opened it. "Was the medicine light?"

"No," Maya said indignantly. "I gave her the prescribed amount." Through gritted teeth, she said, "I've told you repeatedly that her amnesia is total. Why do you keep torturing her?"

Laughing, the man turned and let his eyes bore into the doctor. "How can you say that the amnesia is complete? She knows how to dress herself, she knows how to speak, and she has no problem playing that silly Scrabble game. She must remember something and for me that is unacceptable."

"In other words you want her to be a vegetable."

The man ignored the doctor's words and began pulling wires out of the black bag and placing wire leads of electrodes to specific places on Jane's head.

Jane grabbed the man's hand. "Stop. Stop now."

The man scowled as he turned toward the doctor. "Are you sure you gave her enough medication?" He growled as he began putting the leads back in the case.

"I assure you that she was properly medicated." Maya watched as the man closed the case hard. "I take it you are done with her."

With blazing eyes, the man turned and snarled at the doctor. "We set you up in a world class facility with the best doctors clamoring to be a part of the staff. Do you want that to change?"

Maya shook her head.

"I didn't think so. Don't let this happen again or you will be out looking for a new job with references that will stop anyone from hiring you."

Once the man left the room, Maya stroked Jane's cheek. "You're safe for the moment." She leaned and pressed her lips on Jane's forehead. "There is only so much I can do. Eventually, he will get his way and there will be nothing I can do to stop him. Trust me, I wish I could."

Jane opened her vacant eyes as the door closed.

†

Maya leaned her forehead on a cold window pane. She'd sold her soul to the devil for a few pieces of gold and there was no going back. She cringed every time she had to give Jane a shot of Dilaudid, for it meant that Dr. Spencer Addison would visit the woman and perform a procedure on Jane's brain. She wasn't privy to exactly what or why Addison was doing what he did, but the certainty of the harm he was doing was evident. With each treatment, Jane retreated further into herself. Often before Maya left for home, she'd check on Jane only to see her curled into a fetal position. She also knew that her patient had withdrawn from all social activities and rarely ate. That was in sharp contrast to when she'd first arrived, four months earlier.

Her sanitarium, Salvation, catered to the rich and famous who wanted a place to hide or to recover. Addison and his controlling group would, from time to time, want a patient admitted. All Maya had to do was sign the admittance and release forms. Other than that, Maya had wanted nothing to do with Addison's patients—until Jane arrived.

Jane had come to Salvation under the cloak of darkness. Addison's men swept her into the facility and into a private room and closed the door behind them. The men never stayed longer than a few days and usually left with the patient. Then one day the men were gone, but the patient remained.

When Addison demanded that Maya take the woman on as her patient, she questioned the wisdom of acceptance.

"The new patient we brought in last week claims amnesia. We need her to become your patient. She'll need a complete physical and mental evaluation."

Maya's eyes narrowed. "Exactly what am I looking for?"

"Whether her amnesia claim is legitimate."

"That should be easy enough to determine," Maya countered as she eyed the man. "Surely your own psychiatrists can discover if she's faking or not."

Addison fixed the doctor with his dark gaze. "I believe that our agreement is on a *no questions asked* basis. I expect you to uphold your end of the bargain."

"And I shall."

"See that you do," the man cautioned before disappearing through her office door.

It wasn't until Maya met the woman with the haunted look in her eyes that she knew taking on the woman as her patient was the right thing to do.

Maya had read the report that Addison provided with the woman.

Jane had been found wondering on a roadway, with dried blood in her hair and on her face. In the following medical exam, an unnamed doctor indicated that the woman's head wound was the result of a deep puncture wound. Maya's own examination discovered it was from a surgical procedure.

The woman had no recollection of who she was or where she came from. How she came to be one of Spencer Addison's test subjects was not in the report and Maya knew better than to ask. Whatever he did with the usual people he brought to the sanitarium, it was clear that Jane was different.

Maya gave Jane a complete medical exam, found that the patient, who she estimated was in her early thirties, was five foot seven, and weighed about one hundred and fifteen pounds. Her general condition was malnourished and frail, which made her wonder if they'd starved the woman. In Maya's medical opinion, intense psychoanalysis would have to wait until Jane regained her strength.

As Jane's face and eyes began to show signs of good health, Maya took the woman for walks and got to know her. Once she began psychotherapy, it was quickly apparent that Jane's amnesia was legitimate. Maya saw no evidence in the woman's body language or the words she used that suggested that Jane had any recollection of past events.

Soon after Jane became her patient, Maya found herself drawn to the woman in a way that she didn't understand. Addison called every day for an update on the patient's condition. She felt protective toward Jane who was always holding back about how intensely debilitating her pain was becoming. Maya had cringed, knowing that eventually she'd have to administer stronger drugs and she knew that once that happened, Addison would re-appear. She was certain there was someone on staff that alerted the man to what was going on at Salvation but couldn't pin down who.

Although she didn't have any direct knowledge about what the man did to Jane, she suspected that he was in some way altering her brain function. With each subsequent treatment the woman's pain escalated in strength and frequency. For Maya, *first do no harm* replayed in her mind every time she reported to Addison.

Now, four and a half months later, Jane was still her patient and she had held off Addison as long as possible. He showed up unerringly every time Jane was in pain. She didn't know how he always knew but eventually she'd find out. It wasn't long after Jane was under her care that Maya confirmed to Addison that the woman was indeed an amnesiac and there didn't seem to be any way to change that. The doctor didn't seem to care and gave her specific orders insisting that Jane be treated with powerful pain killers and hallucinogenic medicines. Addison ordered her to make sure the treatment was done in such a manner that the sedation would last several hours.

Maya's musings stopped when her phone rang insistently.

"Dr. Rojas," she said in a clipped tone.

"This is Elinor Scott."

A smile wreathed Maya's full lips. "Dr. Scott, you made it. Did you get everything packed up?"

"Yes, I'm just turning into the property and the moving van is about fifteen minutes behind me."

"Good, once you get all moved in, come to my office."

Maya leaned back in her chair and smiled. She'd liked Elinor Scott from the moment she laid eyes on her. Not only was she talented, she was a beguiling beauty that Maya would like to get to know better. It was no coincidence that Elinor Scott would be living next to her. Maya had arranged it that way by insisting that another staff member move to a different cottage. It had cost her a great deal of her personal money along with the promise of a promotion to get the man and his family to move. Elinor Scott promised to be worth the effort and it was something she didn't regret.

She grinned. "Everything is coming together nicely."

Chapter Six

The tires of an Infinity sedan bumped off the pavement and crunched on gravel as it headed toward a small cottage fifty yards away. Once the vehicle came to a stop, Ellie sat looking at her surroundings as she questioned the wisdom of the move. Resigned to make the best of the situation, she got out of the black car and walked toward the front door.

With the key that had been sent to her, Ellie unlocked the door to the house that would be her new home. When the door opened, her nose immediately took in the smell of cleaning products. As she ventured farther into the empty space, she looked around and sighed. She hoped that taking on the job as medical director at Salvation would be just that—her salvation.

For six months after the mysterious disappearance of Syd, Ellie had drifted in a sea of depression. The world as she knew it no longer existed and life without her wife was simply too hard to bear. For months, she had attempted to pull herself out of the downward spiral. Finally, a chance encounter with a former patient made her realize that she needed to go on.

Rose Montanari, a small woman with a face permanently etched with deep lines, had approached Ellie, who was sitting alone on a park bench.

"Dr. Scott, it is so good to see you again," Rose said, sitting down next to the doctor.

With a vacant stare that turned into recognition, Ellie smiled at the woman. "Mrs. Montanari, it is good to see you again too."

The older woman took the doctor's hand and patted it. "Every night I pray and thank God that you came into my life when you did." Rose smiled. "You saved me—saved my life."

The heartfelt words touched Ellie in a way that no other had in the months since she lost Syd. In that moment of clarity, Ellie knew she needed to pull herself together and begin living again.

The job offer to join the Salvation staff seemed to be exactly what Ellie needed. She would move away from the memories that haunted her. She was making a new start at a new life without Syd. As she looked around the cold, empty room, she questioned the wisdom of her choices.

The honking of a car horn caused Ellie to look out the door. She smiled. Jill was sliding out of her vehicle.

"You made it," Ellie said in a flat tone.

Jill pulled her sister to her and hugged her close. "The moving van is about five minutes behind me." Letting go, Jill looked critically at Ellie's face. "It's going to be okay," she whispered.

"Is it?" Ellie looked away from Jill's intense gaze. "Hiding out here isn't much better than where I was. At least there I could still feel Syd. Here it just seems cold and lonely."

"You're not hiding out here. You have a job and will interact with others. Once we get your things moved in and arranged, it will be a warm, happy place for you."

Ellie shrugged. "I guess."

The two women's attention turned to the rumbling noise of a large truck's engine as it stopped in front of the house.

"Do you need to check in?" Jill asked.

Ellie eyed the man climbing down from the truck's cab. "I called when I got here. Dr. Rojas said to meet her when I was done here."

Jill gently rubbed her hand up and down Ellie's arm. "Why not let me take care of things here."

"Are you sure?" she asked.

The man who got out of the truck walked to the front door. Hank, the driver, who seemed to be in charge, was a burly man dressed in a white coverall. "You need to sign this." He stuck out a clipboard.

Ellie took the paper, read it, and then scribbled her name. "How long will it take to unload the truck?"

Hank rubbed his hand across a stubbly chin. "About two hours to unload. I have a crew that should be here in a little while to unpack for you."

Looking out the door to the truck, Jill frowned. "Are you going to unload it all by yourself?"

With a hearty laugh, the man shook his head. "No." He pointed to the van pulling next to the truck. "My crew just arrived."

Once the men started to move boxes and furniture from the truck into the house, Ellie looked at her sister. "You sure you want to be here alone with them?"

Jill looked at the three men unloading the truck and the four women busily unwrapping kitchen items and smiled. "Yes. You go get your work stuff taken care of and I'll keep an eye on everything here. Are the groceries still in your car?"

Ellie hit her forehead. "Damn! I forgot all about them."

Laughing, Jill hugged her sister. "You go and I'll take care of it. All we can do now is put the cold things away." She eyed the woman busy in the kitchen and laughed again. "If I can get to the refrigerator."

"If you're sure."

"Go," Jill said, as she walked Ellie out the door.

†

After her ten minute walk to the building, Ellie entered the lobby of Salvation and let her eyes run quickly around the area. It was as she remembered when she'd been there for her initial interview. Noting the office of the administrator, she hesitated then made her feet walk toward the reception desk.

"Dr. Scott, you made it," Madeline Spencer said. "It's good to see you again. I'll alert Dr. Rojas that you are here. She picked up the phone and spoke softly into it. "Dr. Scott is here. Yes, I will."

With her heart pounding in her throat, Ellie watched and listened, suddenly terrified that she'd made the wrong decision.

"Dr. Rojas will see you now. Just go ahead to her office."

"Thank you." Ellie walked to the open door and knocked lightly on the door frame.

Dr. Rojas moved out of her chair, frowning slightly. "Dr. Scott, I didn't expect you so soon. Are you already unpacked?"

With a tentative laugh that helped break the apprehension she was feeling, Ellie walked farther into the office. "Hmm, my sister is taking care of that for me."

Maya moved to within inches of her new medical director. "I hope I get to meet her before she leaves." She held out her hand. "I'm glad you're here."

Ellie self-consciously took the administrator's hand and released it after a brief shake. "She's going to stay the week so I'll make sure to introduce her to you."

"Excellent. Come," said Maya. "Let me show you your office now that it has a fresh coat of paint. I think you'll like what we did with it."

†

Ellie looked around the office that was smaller than the administrator's but not by much. The muted green paint set off the cherry desk and bookcase.

"As I told you in your interview, Dr. Scott, the main offices are part of the original structure that was once home to the Lockbourne family estate. Your office was once part of the sitting room." Maya smiled. "I hope you like it."

At a loss for words, Ellie nodded and let a small smile curve her lips. "Yes, it is more than I expected."

The administrator patted the younger doctor's back. "Over here is an area for your consultations with doctors and patients. I've assigned one of the staff members, Inez Greene, to be your intermediary for the time being. At the moment she is at her daughter's school for a parent teacher conference. You will find her knowledgeable and easy to work with. Of course as you settle into the job, I'll welcome all suggestions and feedback you might have."

"Okay," Ellie said tentatively. "Will the intermediary share this office?"

Maya shook her head. "No. Her office is next door. She's been here for seven years and is our HR director. I've asked her to help you get settled and assist you whenever I'm not here and if you have questions."

"Thank you. This is all a bit overwhelming right now." She shrugged. "New home, new job, and all." Ellie looked away when she felt Dr. Rojas' eyes scrutinizing her. She looked back and schooled her features.

"Are you okay?" Maya asked with knitted eyebrows

Ellie nodded. "First day jitters."

"Don't worry. No one here bites." Pointing to the desk, she said, "There is a document you need to sign. I didn't include it in the packet I sent because I need to witness that you signed it."

Ellie nodded again and went to the desk. After she gave the documents a thorough reading, she looked at the administrator in question. "A confidentiality agreement...why? As a doctor I already subscribe to that mindset."

"As I told you during your interview, we have high profile patients who wish to remain anonymous." Maya shrugged. "Their doctors insist that each member of my staff sign that agreement."

Ellie raised her eyebrows, picked up a pen from the desk, and signed the paper. "I'll probably be nervous for a few days."

Maya laughed. "This coming from an ER doctor. I'd think you could handle just about anything that came your way."

Ellie closed her eyes. "Most things, yes, but I've never been a medical director before so it will take some getting used to, Dr. Rojas."

"Maya. Please call me Maya unless we are with a patient."

"Okay." Ellie wasn't interested in being on a first name basis with the woman but at the moment she had no choice.

"Let's see if we can help you along your way to being comfortable here. Come with me and I'll introduce you to the staff and some of the patients. Tomorrow, we will have a proper introduction at the staff's morning breakfast."

With a sense of reluctance, Ellie followed Maya into a corridor that eventually led to the recreation room. The interior of Salvation was as she remembered it, although when there before she had looked more at the lay of the area than at any of the staff or the patients. Now that she was in the room and noticed the patients who were watching television or playing games, it all seemed distressing. She was out of her element and wondered again whether coming there was the wisest choice. Everyone seemed nice enough but Ellie felt like she was one step behind. The headache that rimmed her brain while she walked there was now full blown and all she wanted to do was run away screaming that she'd made a huge mistake.

"Welcome, Dr. Scott. My name is Marie Hendricks and I'm the floor nurse. We were all so excited to learn you would be joining the staff."

Ellie smiled. "Thank you. It will be a challenging job, I'm sure."

"We all try to be advocates for the patients but there are more of them than us. It is good to know you will be here to help us with our most important job—the patients."

"Are there a lot of problems with the patients?" Ellie's interest was piqued.

"For the most part no, but we do have one or two that need special attention."

"When I get settled, I'd like to discuss this further, Marie."

"That will be enough, Marie. Dr. Scott is barely in the door we needn't worry her about such matters now," Maya said.

Ellie saw the look the nurse gave Maya. *Was that fear, apprehension, or hatred?* "Marie, please stop by my office sometime tomorrow."

Marie looked at Dr. Rojas. "I'll try, but sometimes we get really busy and it is hard to get away."

"Okay, then. Whenever you have a chance."

Ellie watched the woman walk away then turned to Maya. "She seems competent and caring. I like to see that in the medical staff."

"Take what Marie says with a grain of salt. She is our resident busybody." Maya looked away. "Please excuse me for a minute. I need to discuss something with one of our nurse's aides."

Ellie looked at the group assembled there and wondered if what Marie said was accurate. Were there patients slipping through the cracks that the staff ignored? She'd have to look into that. Her eyes wandered to where Maya stood speaking to Marie in what looked like a reprimand. *Interesting. Did Marie give away a secret she wasn't supposed to, I wonder?*

Her eyes opened wide when Ellie remembered that her sister was at the cottage sorting through her things. *I'll never find anything if I don't get back there soon.* She made her way to where Maya was still speaking to Marie. She caught the tail end of the conversation.

"...we don't need to be airing our dirty laundry to her yet. Is that clear?"

Ellie cleared her throat and Maya turned around looking like she was caught with her hand in the cookie jar.

So maybe things aren't as pristine as she led me to believe. "Sorry to disturb you, Maya, but I really need to get back to my place. I left my sister there to put things away and I think I need to supervise otherwise I won't find anything once she's gone."

Maya seemed to force a laugh. "That would be a disaster. I'll come by and check on you later if that is all right."

"Certainly. I'll look forward to it." Ellie gave her a weak smile. "Okay, see you later."

She turned and walked away, trying to keep her stride to a walk and not a run—she had to get out of there.

†

When Ellie returned to the cottage, she stood on the threshold and looked at the furniture that was arranged around the open room alongside a multitude of boxes, opened and unopened. Most of the furniture was new but there were some special pieces she brought that reminded her of Syd and when she saw them she began to cry.

"Ellie, what's the matter?"

"I don't know if I can do this."

Jill put her arm around Ellie's shoulders and led her farther into the room, eventually ending up in the bathroom with the door closed. "I thought this is what you wanted."

As her crying became more intense, Ellie began to tremble. "I never got to say goodbye," she sobbed.

"Oh, sweetie, you can't keep torturing yourself like this. Syd is gone and all the tears in the world won't change that."

"The last words I said were *wake me when you get home*. She said she would and then I slept past the time she should have been there." Ellie's body shook with emotion. "If only I woke up at three-thirty maybe she wouldn't be gone now."

With her arms wrapped around her sister, Jill clutched her closer and rocked her gently. "You can't keep living in the past," she whispered. "You need to move on."

"I can't." Ellie held her head. "That place gave me a headache."

"Do you want me to get you something for it?"

"No. Actually when I got out in the fresh air it started to let up some." She swiped at the tears running down her cheeks.

When Ellie's sobs slowed, her sister let her go then looked at her lovingly. "Why don't you give this job a try for three months? If after that, you want to go elsewhere, I'll help you move again."

Ellie nodded. "I'm so glad you are here with me. I feel guilty taking you away from Terry and the kids."

"They love you and understand why I have to be with you now, so no guilty feelings allowed."

Ellie kissed her sister's cheek. "Thank you for everything. I guess we need to go and see what the unpackers are doing. Have you made a list of where everything is?"

Jill laughed and pushed open the door. "Do you know how much stuff you have? It will take all day every day I'm here to get it all arranged."

"Hey, I don't have that much."

Jill raised her eyebrows.

"Okay, maybe I've brought a bit much, but I left a lot of it back at the house."

"There's still a lot of stuff to put away but let me take you on a tour of what I've done so far." Jill grabbed her sister's hand and led her into the kitchen. She opened all the cupboards doors and the drawers. "In this cupboard, I put all your plates and serving dishes."

"Syd gave those to me last year for our anniversary."

"I remember that. She was so anxious that you wouldn't like them. I remember telling her that you'd love anything she gave you."

"You were right." Ellie started closing all the doors and drawers. "I can't do this now."

"No problem. We have all week for you to explore and tell me where you want everything to go."

"We're done now," Hank said, coming into the kitchen. "You need anything else before we go?"

Ellie shook her head, fished a hundred dollar bill out of her wallet, and handed it to the man. "No, we're good. Thank you for everything."

Hank took the bill and nodded. "Ever need movers again, call us and I'll make sure you get a really good deal." Hank tipped his baseball cap and he and his crew left the house.

Closing the door, Jill patted Ellie's shoulder. "How was your visit to Salvation?"

"You will have to come see the office they gave me. It is huge and I'm pretty sure that all the furniture is Stickley in cherry."

"Classy. Sounds like they spared no expense." Jill smiled. "Did you meet any of the staff or patients?"

Ellie frowned.

"I don't like that look. What's the matter?" Jill asked.

"There was one floor nurse who was very friendly and she was telling me that sometimes they have problems with patients. Then Dr. Rojas came up and told her she'd said enough and then a little while later I saw her chewing the nurse out."

"Really. I wonder why."

"I overheard a little of the conversation and Dr. Rojas said something about not airing dirty laundry or something like that." Ellie shook her head. "And I had to sign a confidentiality agreement. Something about high profile patients. I think that is code for movie or rock stars."

"Stars? Did you know that before?"

"She said she'd mentioned it but I don't remember that."

"What do you...."

A soft knock on the door sounded.

Ellie sighed. "I can't handle visitors. Can you get that?"

"Sure. Make yourself scarce and I'll see who it is."

Jill walked to the front door, opened it, and stared at a tall woman with black hair and equally dark eyes. "Hi, can I help you?"

"You must be Elinor's sister. I'm Maya Rojas." The administer smiled and held out a bottle of wine. "Since I live next door, I wanted to give your sister a proper welcome."

"Please come in, Dr. Rojas."

"Please call me Maya. Dr. Rojas sounds so formal."

Jill smiled and gestured to the couch. "Please take a seat and I'll see what's happened to Ellie."

"Ellie. Is that what I should call your sister and not Elinor?"

"You should probably ask her." Jill smiled, "I'll be right back."

Jill pushed the bedroom door open and saw Ellie sitting on the bed with her head in her hands.

"Who was it?"

"Dr. Rojas is here."

"Why? What does *she* want?"

"She came to welcome you with a bottle of wine.

"Tell her I'm sick, have a headache, or anything so she will go away."

Jill sucked in a breath to temper her growing annoyance. "No. She came here to welcome you to your new home so you will go out there and be nice. This isn't like you. You're not a rude person."

Ellie glared.

"Don't give me that look. To move here was your decision, Ellie, and your boss has come to welcome you. Now get your butt up off that bed, go wash your face, and then go out and be a gracious hostess."

"Fine but she isn't going to stay that long, so don't go asking her to sit down and visit. I'll say thank you and goodbye at the same time."

"You will not. That isn't who you are and I can't believe you would ever consider being ungracious."

Ellie lowered her head. "I can't do this," she whispered. "It's too much, too soon."

Jill moved and wrapped her arms around Ellie's head and pulled her close. "Yes, you can. You've started. Don't turn back now. It will get easier once you get caught up in your job. Please, for me, make an effort and be sociable."

"Okay. I'll be out in a minute. I need to pull myself together."

†

"Looks like you two have a lot of work to do before this is a home," Maya said when Jill returned.

"Once Ellie decides where she wants everything it won't take long." Jill smiled. "She had a bit of a headache so she was laying down. She'll be out in a few minutes."

Maya's face went flat. "Oh, I didn't want you to wake her."

"It's okay, she wasn't sleeping, just resting." Jill waved her hand around the room. "Besides, she has work to do and can't just lounge around all day."

"Do you need some help? I can see if I can round up some people to help out."

"No, that won't be necessary. This place isn't that big and we've got all the heavy stuff arranged. The rest should be done in a few days."

"Of course once that is done it will be time to rearrange." Maya smiled.

"Isn't that how it always goes?" Jill laughed. "I've been in my home for seven years and am still moving things around."

Both women were laughing when Ellie came into the room. "What's so funny?" she asked, frowning.

Jill winked at her sister. "I was telling Maya about all the work you have to do in getting this place livable."

"Mmhmm. I thought that's why I brought you along."

"Look what Maya brought you." Jill said holding up the bottle of wine. "Shall I get some glasses?"

"Oh, none for me," Maya said, standing up. "I need to get back to my house. I just wanted to let you know how pleased I am that you have joined the staff Elinor, or should I call you Ellie?"

"I'd prefer Elinor."

"Elinor it is then." Maya smiled. "If you need anything at all, please don't hesitate to ask." She pointed to the right. "I'm right next door and my cupboards are full, so don't be shy."

For a moment Ellie closed her eyes recalling what her sister said about being hospitable. "Please stay and share a glass of wine with us." She looked at the bottle and saw a familiar label. "How did you know Black Bear Chardonnay is one of my favorites?"

Maya smiled, seemingly pleased that her selection was the correct one. "I really need to get back. I put a pot roast in the crockpot this morning and if I don't get to it soon, it will be nothing but mush." Her eyes widened. "You know, I have enough for an army so why don't you both share it with me?"

Jill looked at her sister. "We'd love to." She held up the wine bottle. "We can bring the wine."

"Wonderful. Why don't you come in about an hour. By then I'll have everything ready."

Once Maya was gone, Ellie glared at her sister. "Why did you tell her that? I don't want to go."

"Sure you do, Ellie, you just don't know it yet."

Ellie's frown deepened.

"You said you'd give it three months. This is your start so don't wimp out before you even begin."

Ellie set her jaw. "I'm not wimping out. I just didn't want to have dinner with her."

"Why?"

"Because she's the boss."

Jill lightly punched her sister's arm. "That's stupid. Right now, she's your next door neighbor who is welcoming you. Now, pull yourself together and get ready. We're having pot roast for dinner."

†

When she heard the knock on her door, Maya smiled. She was glad the sisters had accepted her offer. Her plan when she started the crockpot that morning was to invite Elinor to dinner. She didn't know at the time about Jill being there too, but she had enough food for at least five people. Elinor Scott was intelligent and would be a welcome addition to a staff that she often found lacking, as far as someone she could relate to. She saw sadness in the new medical director's eyes but she was certain that with the right approach she could find out the why, fix it, and draw Elinor closer to her.

"Hi," Maya said opening the door. "I am so happy you both could join me."

"Thank you for the invite." Jill elbowed her sister.

"It smells delicious." Ellie smiled. "My mouth is watering already."

The robotic sound of Elinor's voice made Maya wonder if she'd done something wrong. "Welcome. Come on in and make yourself at home. I just need a few minutes to toss the salad." Maya looked at the wine bottle Jill was holding out. She pointed to a cabinet on the far wall. "There's a corkscrew there with wine glasses. Would you please do the honors, Elinor?"

Ellie's eyebrows creased. "Sure."

Maya nodded. "I'll be right back."

"Can I help with anything?" Jill asked.

"Thanks, but no. I've got it all done. Please take a seat."

Once Maya left the room Jill nudged Ellie. "What was that look for? All she did was ask you to pour the wine. Come on, get with the program."

"Fine, but I'm not staying long."

Much to her surprise, the meal was enjoyable for Ellie. While they talked, she found Maya to be witty with a wicked sense of humor. She certainly wasn't the tight ass that Ellie had expected from someone in her position. She guessed, by where she was career wise, that Maya was in her early fifties although she certainly didn't look that old. Her body wasn't sculptured by any means, for it showed the signs of someone who sits at a desk all the time, but she had all the right curves and was fit in a soft sort of way. It was her personality that Ellie found—how did she find it— *enchanting* was the word that came to her mind.

"So what did you do after he dumped his oatmeal in your lap?" Jill asked.

Maya laughed. "I took a spoon, scraped it off my trousers, and put it back in the bowl. Then I said, *I take it you don't like your breakfast.*"

When both Jill and Maya began to laugh harder, Ellie smiled and wondered what the joke was. She let out a small laugh of her own to cover her embarrassment of not listening. "Sounds like I'll have my work cut out for me."

Maya patted Ellie's shoulder. "Not with him. He's no longer at our facility."

"Oh. Then he got better. That is good to hear."

"Unfortunately, he checked himself out. Last I heard the family had a full time caretaker for him." Maya shook her head. "It is disappointing when all our efforts don't help our patients. I'm of the school that there is always something we can do to better our patients' lives."

Ellie nodded. "I agree. That is the most frustrating part in medicine—when you've run out of options and there is nothing left to do but make your patient comfortable."

"I know that feeling well," Maya said.

"The pot roast was delicious," Jill offered.

"Yes, it was," Ellie added.

"Thank you both. I'm so glad you were able to join me. It gets lonely eating alone all the time." Maya shrugged. "Often I'll take my meals at Salvation. The food is fabulous and there are other people to sit with."

"I'll have to remember that." Ellie looked at her watch. "We really should go. Those boxes won't get unpacked by themselves."

70

"Let me help you clean up first," Jill said."

Maya waved her hand. "Not necessary. There isn't that much and I know how tedious unpacking can be. Best get it all done then you two can relax and enjoy your time together."

Ellie pushed back her chair and stood. "Thank you again for the meal. It was delicious."

"Maybe we can do it again." Maya stood.

"We'll see." There was no way Ellie was going to commit to having dinner with the woman. Yes, she was an interesting person but she had no intention of getting involved in a friendship or a dinner partner. She wasn't about to betray Syd with Maya or anyone else. Ellie held out her hand. "Thank you again."

Maya took the offered hand and gave it a squeeze. "You're more than welcome. Please don't be a stranger. We are neighbors after all."

Ellie nodded and started for the door. "Jill, are you coming."

"I feel guilty leaving Maya with all the dishes," Jill said. "You go on ahead and I'll be there after I help."

"Nonsense. I am perfectly capable of doing the dishes myself and if the truth be known, I have a certain way I like to do them." Maya smiled. "No offense meant."

"None taken. If you're sure...."

"I am."

"Okay, then. Thank you for the meal and I hope I'll see you again before I leave, Maya."

"I'd like that."

Once back inside the cottage, Jill grinned at her sister. "She likes you."

Ellie frowned. "What?"

"Maya likes you."

"No, she doesn't. She's my boss."

"So what. I'm telling you she likes you."

Ellie cocked her head. "You really think so?"

"Are you completely blind? She didn't take her eyes off you all through dinner…and before."

"It's too soon. What if Syd comes back?"

"Ellie, remember why you're here. You came to get away from the memories and for a new start." Jill saw the apprehension in her sister's eyes. "Just give it a chance, okay."

"We'll see." Ellie scrubbed her hand across her face. "I need a shower."

Chapter Seven

The next morning, Ellie walked into her office carrying a box of personal items that her sister insisted she take to make the office her own. As far as she was concerned, none of it mattered for she wouldn't be there that long. For the next three months, she would do her job, then politely tender her resignation.

Ellie tore through the box looking for a picture of Syd. When she didn't find one she dialed Jill's cell number. "Where's my picture of Syd?" Ellie blurted, as soon as she heard her sister's voice.

"I didn't put one in the box."

"Why?" Ellie demanded.

"Look, this is your new start and you need to go forward and not backward."

"That isn't your choice to make," Ellie shouted.

Maya poked her head in the office. "Is everything okay, Elinor?"

Ellie glared at Maya then sighed. "Yes, just a disagreement with my sister."

Maya nodded. "When you're finished I need you in the lounge we're having a welcome breakfast for you."

Ellie nodded. "Give me a couple of minutes and I'll be right there."

"Take your time." Maya smiled and closed the door.

"I need to go. Apparently they are having some sort of welcome breakfast." Ellie tried but couldn't keep the growl out of her voice.

"Ellie, I'm sorry. I can find a picture and bring it to you if you want."

Blowing out a breath, Ellie closed her eyes. "No. I'll find one when I get back there. I've got to go and have breakfast with strangers."

"Give them a chance. You might find a friend or two."

"You don't get it, do you, Jill. I doubt you ever will."

Ellie ended the call and stood. "Showtime," she muttered.

†

After shaking everyone's hand and trying to remember their names, Ellie felt her shoulders tensing as if they were reaching for her jawline. Soon she was speaking with several women who had friendly faces and seemed to want to take her under their wings—she found that both annoying and touching.

The nurse she met the day before, Marie approached her. "Dr. Scott, I hope I didn't give you the wrong impression yesterday. We do have some patients that need more attention than others but this is an excellent facility and I am proud to work here."

Ellie smiled. She liked the woman who seemed to be genuinely interested in the patients and doing a good job. "Not to worry, I have worked enough hospital shifts to know that in spite of what you do there will always be a problem or two. Once I get settled, I am going to invite some of the staff to sit down with me and get their take on what their role is in conjunction with the patients."

"I'd like that. I've never worked any place where anyone really wanted my input. I'm so glad you're here," Marie gushed.

"Talk with you later."

Ellie moved away, her eyes darting to the exit, wondering when she could get away. *Won't be soon enough.* She frowned. Damn, they hadn't even eaten yet. It was going to be a long morning.

"Are you getting acquainted with the staff?" Maya asked.

"Yes, I am. They seem like a friendly group. I'm thinking that after I've familiarized myself with the inner workings of Salvation, I'll set up meetings with each individual medical staff member and find out their thoughts and needs."

"That sounds excellent. I think you will find all the staff to be top notch. It sounds to me like you want to take a hands on approach with your job." Maya smiled. "I like that way of thinking. Our last medical director, Robert Morton, was more of a director than a people person."

Ellie thought for a moment. *People person? Me? Yeah I guess that's true...or it used to be.* "I can't imagine doing this type of job and not taking the time to interact with the staff. I consider that essential."

"As do I." Maya looked at someone coming in the door. "Oh, there is David Caruthers our chief of psychiatry." She took Ellie's hand. "Come on, you need to meet him."

Despite Ellie's attempt to shake her hand free and walk unaided, Maya held on tight. When they reached the man, Ellie attempted to contain her annoyance with Maya and not take it out on this man.

"David, I'm glad you could make it," Maya said. "This is Elinor Scott, our new medical director."

David held out his hand. "It's a pleasure to meet you, Elinor."

"Likewise." Ellie studied the man. He was tall—at least six two she guessed—bald, with thick glasses over his brown eyes. His grip was firm but not excessively so. It was his smile that drew Ellie in immediately. It was warm and inviting and for the first time since she'd arrived there she felt her shoulders relax. *If he has that kind of effect on me he must be very good at his job.* "I'm eager to get your ideas about what you see as your mission and that of your staff."

"Ah, proactive, I see. I like that. I think we will work very well together, Elinor."

"Yes, I believe that too." Ellie gave the man a sincere smile.

"It looks like they are ready to serve breakfast. Please sit with us, David. That way you and Elinor can get better acquainted."

†

Ellie closed the file she was reading on her computer and sighed. The day had been long and she was exhausted. Her phone chirped and she saw that it was a text from Jill.

Hey, I just ordered a pizza with the works. It should be here in 30 minutes. Any idea when you will get home?

Just finishing up now. I should be there before the pizza. You did get anchovies, didn't you?

Of course. See you soon.

Ellie smiled. The running joke between Jill, Syd, and herself was anchovies on pizza. Any time they'd order pizza Syd would always remind them not to forget the anchovies. Back when Syd and Ellie were first dating, the subject of anchovies came up when Syd asked for them on her pizza. Both Jill and Ellie turned up their noses and said *yuck,* offering to get Syd her own pizza. It was then that Syd started to laugh and eventually they were all laughing with tears rolling down their cheeks. Syd finally managed to say *I don't like anchovies either* and they all began to laugh more.

The memory was like a knife was stabbed into her heart. "God, what I wouldn't give to have you here with me now."

Just then there was a soft knock on her door before it opened. Maya was standing there with a smile on her face.

"It's time to call it a day, Elinor. Get your things and walk with me to your home and you can tell me about your day."

Maya's voice was so soft and compelling that Ellie nodded and pushed away from her desk. "Sounds good to me, I think we are both going the same way." She smiled and her reward was a warm welcoming look.

"I believe we are."

Once the two women were outside walking toward the cottages, Maya spoke again. "How did your first day go?"

"To tell you the truth, I'm exhausted. It will take me a month of Sundays to get through all the paperwork the former director left behind."

"Do you need some help? Did you get together with Inez?"

"Yes, she was very helpful but it is the volume that is daunting."

"Have you thought about just disregarding all his papers and starting out new?"

"Yes, but I think I should at least scan his notes in case there is something important that I should know."

They had reached the cottages and Maya took Ellie's arm. "I'll clear my schedule for Thursday and we can have a brain storming session. What do you say?"

"That sounds good to me."

At that moment a car with a Pete's Pizza sign on the side pulled up.

"It's the best pizza around," Maya said.

Ellie closed her eyes and resigned herself to what she had to do. "You want to join us?" she said as brightly as possible.

Maya smiled. "Thank you, but no. I still have roast to eat and right now all I want to do is take a hot bath."

"That sounds heavenly." Ellie looked around wondering who said the words only to realize they came from her mouth. Her face went instantly red and she was grateful that the kid delivering the pizza chose that moment to announce his presence.

"See you tomorrow, Maya," Ellie said as she crooked her finger at the young man. "Follow me."

†

"Watcha doin'?" Jill asked while standing in the doorway of the bedroom Ellie was using.

"I'm looking for Syd's picture. I know I packed it."

"Let me help." Jill moved into the room and opened a box. "Which one are you looking for?"

"The one of her sitting on a boulder in the Grand Teton National Park."

Jill smiled. "I always liked that one of her."

Ellie put her hand in a box then lifted it out triumphantly with the picture in hand. "Found it." She looked at it longingly. "She is so beautiful."

Jill sucked in a breath not knowing what to say to her sister that wouldn't make her mad. "Ellie, do they know you're a lesbian at Salvation?'

Ellie's head snapped up. "What business is it of theirs? None!"

"Didn't you say you were going to have all the medical staff come and visit with you in your office."

"So."

"If they see the picture on your desk it won't be much of a leap for them to guess your sexual preferences. Do you have any idea what the policy is for sexual orientation at Salvation?"

"No."

Jill felt her sister's eyes bore into her and she shivered. *In for a penny in for a pound.* "This is your chance for a new start..." She held her hand up when Ellie opened her mouth. "For the time being you need to concentrate on your job. People are depending on you so you can't let anything distract you."

"How can a picture of Syd distract me?" Ellie asked in a growl. "I need to have her there with me."

Jill moved closer and knelt down in front of her sister. "Ellie, she is always with you in your heart and mind. You don't need a picture of her to feel her near."

"I do too."

"No. Having the picture on your desk will be a distraction for you." Jill lifted Ellie's chin. "You know I'm right. If you have it there now, people will ask who she is and then you will have to dredge up the story and tell it again and again. Every time you talk about Syd it tears at your heart. Is that what you want—to relive that day and the days since in front of strangers?"

Ellie was crying. "No. I couldn't bear it."

"Then why don't you give yourself time to get into the routine of your job and not share Syd with anyone for now." Jill handed Ellie a tissue. "You have her picture on your phone right."

Ellie nodded.

"When you feel the need to see her, look there for now."

Running fingers through her hair, Ellie shook her head. "I don't want to be here."

"I know but you said you'd give it three months."

"And I will." Ellie wrapped her arms around Jill's shoulders. "Whatever am I going to do when you leave."

"I'll be but a phone call away. We can have video chats and we will see you every weekend. You won't be alone ever."

"I love you, Jill. Thank you for being here with me."

"I'll always be here for you. Come on. I think I heard cold pizza calling our names."

†

Ellie was going through the mound of files from her predecessor, grumbling, when she looked up to see Maya standing in the doorway. "Hi, come on in."

"Am I interrupting?"

"No. Inez is helping me sort through these notes and I think I am finally getting a handle on them." Ellie forced a smile. "Is there something I can help you with?"

"Yes. I need your advice." Maya sat in the chair next to Ellie's desk and let out a sigh. "What do you know about pain management?"

Lifting her eyebrows, Ellie looked at her boss. "Are you looking for the answer from a psychiatric or a medical doctor point of view?"

"Medical."

"May I ask in what context you are coming from?"

Maya smiled and shrugged. "I have a patient who had a brain injury that resulted in amnesia."

"Complete?"

"Yes. She presents with severe headaches and always waits until they are debilitating before she asks for help. I'd like to come up with a medication regimen that would stave off the extreme pain." She lifted her shoulders. "I don't want to have to give her Demerol, Dilaudid, or morphine unless absolutely necessary."

"Wow, the pain *must* be debilitating if you have to use those drugs. Where does the pain first begin?"

"The patient has a surgical scar here," Maya pointed to her medial temporal lobe, "That seems to be where the pain originates."

"I assume you have done a CAT scan."

"Yes, and there is nothing that shows up as something that would cause pain like that."

"Hmm. I've had success with low dose amitriptyline—say fifty milligrams—in conjunction with a pain med such as Darvocet, Vicodin, or, if needed Oxycodone. The patient will still be loopy with those drugs but the affect won't be as debilitating as giving her Demerol and the like."

"Why the antidepressant?" Maya asked.

Taking off her glasses, Ellie smiled at the woman. "In blind studies they found that a low dose of an antidepressant helps chronic pain. There's also Gabapentin but that is more for nerve pain."

"Interesting. And you say you've had success with that method of treatment?"

81

"For the most part. As you know, it is often difficult to distinguish between actual physical pain and what the mind perceives as pain."

The administrator stood. "Thanks, I'll give that a try." Maya was almost out the door when she turned back. "Elinor, I'm really glad you're here."

Ellie smiled. "Tomorrow morning Jill is leaving. Is it okay if I come in late?"

Maya nodded and smiled. "You are the medical director, Elinor, you don't have to ask for permission."

"Okay, thanks."

"I really like Jill. She is a wonderful person. It would be my pleasure to take both of you out to dinner tonight if that isn't being too pushy."

Ellie thought about how to say *no* in a tactful way that was nice before she heard Jill telling her to be more approachable. "Sure, we'd love it."

"Great. I'll make reservations at this great steak house I know. I'll pick you both up around six."

Ellie nodded and when the door closed she buried her face in her hands. "I should have said *no*."

Chapter Eight

Ellie had been working at Salvation for four weeks and found herself liking the job and the people who worked there, despite her earlier misgivings. Maya, especially, was a surprise to her. She initially had doubts but as it turned out Maya was both charming and supportive.

Ellie still went home every weekend and drove the lonely stretch of road hoping to find Syd. She took comfort in her family and the strong bond she shared with Syd's parents.

During the work week, she'd meet with Maya and discuss what she was doing and tweak her approach to the job. So far she had met with all of the staff and found them to be dedicated and capable. Her biggest challenge now was to observe all the medical staff at work.

"Do you think I should inform the staff that I'll be observing them?" Ellie asked Maya.

"No. Why would you?"

"It is important to me that they know that it is part of my job and in no way reflects on them or their work ethic. I remember when I had evaluations and it made me hyper-vigilant and I don't want that to happen. I've found that all hyper-vigilance does is cause mistakes.

"Yes, I'd agree with that. Unfortunately, no matter what you say, they will be wary when you are there to evaluate them. It is the nature of the beast, I'm afraid."

Ellie nodded. "Guess I'll have to think of a way to observe and not be seen as observing."

Maya, who was sitting next to Ellie, smiled. "If anyone can do that, it is you. By the way, thanks for dinner last night. I'd never have pegged you as a gourmet cook. I think I had dreams of your chicken Kiev last night."

"Really?" Ellie raised an eyebrow. "Would you like the leftovers?"

"I'd love them."

"Thanks for taking them. I'm not much of a leftovers kind of gal. I had enough of them when I was an intern to last a lifetime."

"I hear you."

Ellie zoned out for a minute as she recalled the previous night's dinner with Maya. They did have a good time and they laughed, which felt good. It had been a long time since she remembered a genuine laugh. The most disturbing part of the night was when Maya was leaving. It was so unexpected—Maya leaning in and kissing her. Ellie had pulled away immediately but still saw the look on Maya's face. It was a mix between bewilderment and rejection. *I can't do that*, she recalled saying to Maya before closing the door. Her ears perked up when she heard a change in Maya's tone and she listened to what was being said.

"Listen, I have to go to Sacramento for a meeting with the shareholders on Wednesday," Maya told Elinor. "I am going to need you to be on call should anything arise. I don't foresee that happening but you never know."

"How long will you be gone?" Ellie looked away, astonished that knowing Maya would not be there made her sad.

"Two days tops. They usually schmooze the attendees with dinners and an evening at the symphony."

"Do you like going to the symphony?"

"Yes. Yes, I do. I like getting dressed up and going out on the town. There really isn't an opportunity to do that here." Maya smiled. "Are you a symphony kinda girl?"

"Can't say since I've never been to one. I do like classical music though."

"Well, we will have to change that. When I get back we can plan on introducing you to the world of the symphony." Maya looked away. "About last night...I'm sorry. I shouldn't have kissed you."

"It isn't you that should be sorry. It's me. You caught me off guard, that's all." This wasn't the time to get into a discussion about Syd. Ellie shrugged. "Back to you leaving...I haven't seen you rushing out at all hours of the night so I think I'll be okay watching things."

"Great. The night staff is really great so I don't foresee any problems for you. I remember once leaving Robert in charge and when I got back there were so many complaints that it sealed his dismissal."

"I won't let you down."

"I never considered that you would." Maya smiled and touched Ellie's arm.

The shiver that went through her body made Ellie suck in a deep breath as she fell into Maya's eyes.

"When I get back would you go out to dinner with me?" Maya asked in a sultry voice.

Ellie swallowed hard. Her mind was screaming *no* but her body was saying *yes*. "I'd like that."

Maya's smile broadened. "I'll be looking forward to it."

†

Late the next afternoon, after Maya had been gone for most of the day, a man with white hair barged into Ellie's office.

"May I help you?" Ellie said, glaring at the man.

The man gave her an admittance form. "You need to sign that."

With her eyebrows knitting, Ellie looked at the form then back at the man. "I can't sign this. This isn't my patient. You have to get the signature of the admitting physician."

With his hands planted flat on Ellie's desk, the man leaned into her. "The arrangement is that Dr. Rojas signs in my patients. Since she's not here, it falls on you." He pierced the doctor with a malevolent gaze. "This is not up for discussion."

Straightening her back, Ellie matched the man's gaze. "I will not admit this patient. You will have to go through the proper channels."

The man let out an audible growl as he pulled a cell phone out of his pocket and dialed a number.

"The woman you left in charge refuses to sign an admittance form."

With a sneer, the man shoved his phone in Ellie's direction.

With a tentative motion, Ellie took the phone. "Hello."

"Elinor, I need you to go ahead and sign the form."

"I can't without at least examining the patient."

"Please, sign the paper and I'll explain when I return."

Ellie's eyes narrowed. "It goes against everything I believe in."

"I understand your misgivings. Believe me, I do, but at this moment you need to sign the paper."

Hearing the tremor in Maya's voice made Ellie pause for a moment. "Why?"

"Just sign the damn paper, Elinor," Maya barked.

Ellie picked up a pen and scribbled her name next to the box that said attending physician and when the man looked away she scribbled *under duress* below her signature.

The man snatched his phone from the doctor's grip. "It's done," he said before closing the phone and walking out of Ellie's office.

"What was that all about?" Ellie was tempted to call Maya back and demand an explanation.

How dare she order me to sign the admittance form!

She was raging inside and picked up her phone. "Hello, Inez, will you please come to my office at your earliest convenience?"

"Is something wrong?"

"Yes."

"I'll be right there."

The light rap on the door made Ellie let out the breath she was holding. "Come in."

"What's up," Inez asked.

"You're the only person I trust to talk with this about."

"Sounds serious."

"I think it is but I have no frame of reference to determine what the right thing to do is. As head of HR, I thought you'd know."

A warm smile crossed Inez's face. She was probably in her mid-thirties, of medium build with dark auburn hair, grey eyes, and a smile that lit up a room. "Tell me what it is and we can solve it together."

Ellie closed her eyes and sighed. "Some man came barging into my office a little while ago demanding I sign an admittance form."

Inez's eyes widened. "Do you know who he was?"

"No. I've never seen him before. When I refused to sign, he made a call."

"Really?" Inez's brow wrinkled. "Who was it?"

"Maya."

"Did you speak to her?"

"Oh, yes. He shoved the phone in my face and when I realized who it was, she told me to sign the form. I voiced my objections and told her I didn't understand what was going on."

"Then what?"

"I think the man frightened her. She ordered me to sign the paper." Ellie shrugged. "I had no choice so I signed the paper."

"Sounds like that was the right move at the time. Had it been me, I think I'd be terrified. Did you speak with Maya further?"

"No. She did tell me she'd explain when she got back. It better be for a damn good reason because I could lose my medical license over this." Ellie gritted her teeth. "It wasn't my patient and I didn't even have the chance to examine the person. The man just roared in here demanding that I admit a patient that I knew nothing about."

"You definitely have grounds to file a grievance, but if you do you will have to admit you signed that form."

"I put *under duress* below my name. He was so angry and in a rush I doubt he saw that."

"Smart thinking. Hopefully he won't notice. Otherwise he may come back."

"I'm caught in a Catch 22. Any suggestions?"

"Lock your door after I leave, for starters." Inez nodded in what looked like contemplation. "When will Maya return?"

"Mid-afternoon Friday."

"As soon as she gets here, let me know and I'll be there with you to talk to her about this incident. I've worked with her for many years and she has always been above board and a stickler for rules. Whatever this is, she must have had a good reason. Of that I'm sure."

"Thank you, Inez. You've been invaluable to me this past month. I trust your advice and will wait for Maya to return before I take any further action."

"You are not alone in this, Elinor."

Ellie finally let a smile curve her lips. "Having your support helps. Thanks again.

Once Inez left her office, Ellie locked the door before going back to her desk and burying her face in her hands. It irked her no end that she was forced to compromise her principles and her position. She would get to the bottom of it even if it meant she'd resign earlier than planned.

†

After a long day fraught with problems, Ellie sat on her couch with a glass of wine in hand. She was still smarting from Maya's demand and tried to put it out of her mind. *There is nothing I can do about it now.*

Her phone rang and thought perhaps it was Maya calling to explain. When she looked at the caller ID she saw it was someone at Salvation calling. "Dr. Scott."

"This is Mary O'Brian. One of Dr. Rojas patients is in need of medical help."

"What is the problem?"

"Jane had a brain injury that can at times cause her tremendous pain…that is happening now."

Remembering the discussion she had with Maya about the patient, Ellie set her wine glass down. "I'll be right there."

Moments later, entering the darkened room, Ellie turned on the light. She saw a woman sitting on a bed with her arms wrapped around her bent legs and her head buried in her knees.

"Turn the light off!" the woman cried.

Snapping the switch down, Ellie ventured toward the woman. "I'm Dr. Scott."

"I need Dr. Rojas," a trembling voice said.

"She's not here. Let me help you," Ellie soothed.

When the woman lifted her head, Ellie let out an audible gasp. "It can't be," she whispered. "Is it really you?"

Jane looked at the woman in question. "Do I know you?"

Tears were streaming down Ellie's cheeks as she pulled the woman into her arms. "Syd," she whispered.

Struggling to free herself, Jane pushed the doctor away. "Get away from me," she growled. "I want Dr. Rojas."

Ellie tried to squelch the trembling of her heart. The woman had no idea of who she was or what they meant to one another. If she was going to help her, she needed to put on her doctor's hat and help with the problem at hand—the debilitating headache.

"Jane, Dr. Rojas is not here but she told me what to do to help your pain."

The patient put her hands up to her head. "I thought I could control it," she cried.

Ellie put her hand over one of Jane's. *That's so like you.* "I know. That's why I brought you some medication to make it go away."

Terror seemed to fill Jane's eyes. "No drugs," she shouted. "If you give me the shot, that man will come."

"What man?" Ellie asked.

"The one with the white hair," Jane said, in a quivering voice,

White hair? Can it be the same man? "Not tonight," Ellie said in a firm tone. "Roll over and let me give you the shot." Once Jane complied, Ellie pulled a chair to the bed and sat down. "No one is going to hurt you ever again," she whispered. "You won't be alone, I'll be here all night."

When the door rattled, then opened, Ellie sat up, and looked at a figure standing in the threshold. It was the same man she'd encountered earlier in the day.

"Get out," Ellie ordered as she positioned herself between the man and the patient that she now knew was Syd.

The man moved farther into the room. "You have no right to tell me that." The man snarled as he approached the bed.

"Leave or I'll call security."

With a bellowing laugh, the man pushed past her. "It's your turn to leave."

Ellie walked rapidly to the door. "Someone get security in here immediately," she called out. When she saw a nurse pick up the phone, she turned back to the man and Syd. Her mouth flew open when she saw the man attaching electrodes from a small black case—it resembled a doctor's bag—to the patient's head. "Stop that immediately!" she ordered.

The man with white hair ignored her and continued with his task.

Grabbing the man's arm, Ellie pulled on it only to have the man easily push her away.

"Stop what you're doing right now!" she screamed. She grabbed the black case containing the electrodes and pulled it away.

When the wire leads pulled off Syd's head, the man turned and slapped Ellie, sending her to the floor.

Staff and patients crowded around the open door. One nurse, Bill Murkowski came into the room and pulled the man away from the bed. Just then, two security officers pushed their way into the room and looked at Ellie who was getting up from the floor.

Ellie pointed to the man with white hair. "Get him out of here. He doesn't belong here."

The two officers grabbed the man and escorted him out of the room. "You'll be sorry you did this," he snarled as he was hustled out.

"The show's over," Ellie said, looking at the people standing at the door, She smiled at Bill and closed her eyes. "Thanks for coming in when you did."

Bill moved closer to the doctor. "You're bleeding."

Ellie touched her lip and felt the stickiness then tasted the coppery taste of blood. "Do me a favor and catch the security guys and tell them to call the police.

After the nurse left the room, Ellie turned toward Syd who was cowering under the covers. "It's okay now, Jane. That man will never hurt you again.

Terrified familiar hazel eyes peered out from under the sheet. "How can you say that?"

Ellie rubbed her eyes and looked at the black case still sitting by the bed. "Has he used that before?"

Syd nodded.

Ellie pulled the remaining electrodes off Syd's head and packed them into the black case before closing it. "Does Dr. Rojas allow him to hurt you?" Ellie asked with her anger rising.

"She said just like you that she wouldn't let him hurt me but he still comes in here and puts those things on my head."

Looking at the woman called Jane, Ellie saw her beloved Syd and fought the urge to hold her close and kiss her. She sat in the chair next to the bed. "Go to sleep. You're safe now."

A nurse crept into the room and touched Ellie's shoulder. "The police are here. They want to know what you want to do with that man."

Ellie nodded and gave the woman a brief grateful smile. "I'll be right there. Can you stay with her until I return, Libby?"

"Sure, let me tell my floor nurse."

"Thank you." Once the nurse left the room, Ellie stood and bent down to put her lips near Syd's ear. "Return to me," she whispered before she kissed Syd's cheek.

†

The man with the white hair, flanked by two police officers, stood in the Atrium. When Ellie approached them the man sneered at her. "You have no right to detain me."

"What's your name again?" Ellie asked knowing that the question would irritate the man.

With a scowl the man said, "Dr. Spencer Addison. I'd think you'd remember from the admission earlier."

Ellie ignored his comment and walked to a computer at the reception desk, logged in, and accessed the employee database.

"Dr. Addison, if you are indeed a doctor, I don't see your name as someone who has privileges at Salvation. Therefore your being here and attempting to treat a patient who is not under your care is illegal." She rubbed a hand across her face.

"I have every right," the man countered. "Just ask Dr. Rojas."

"That is really not relevant. You attacked me," she pointed to her split lip. "So I am going to file a complaint against you."

"You can't do that!"

Ellie smiled and looked at the officers. "What do I have to do to file the complaint for assault?" She recalled all the staff standing in the doorway witnessing the man's attack on her. "And I can provide witnesses."

"You'll have to come to the police station and sign the complaint," a burly police officer said.

"I'm in charge here so I can't just leave right now," Ellie said. "I don't suppose someone could bring it to me."

The younger of the two officers smiled. "Once we've done the paper work, I'll bring the form back for you to sign."

"Thank you." She looked at Addison. "What will happen to him?"

"We will hold him until he sees the judge."

Ellie nodded. "Thank you for everything." She glared at the white haired man. "I don't want to see you anywhere near that patient or any of our patients again. If I do, I'll make sure you are charged with much more than assault."

Addison snorted. "No, you won't." He lifted a shoulder and grinned.

Not wanting the man to know he unnerved her, Ellie turned away. "I'm done speaking to you."

The police took Addison away and Ellie returned to Syd's room.

"Thank you for staying with her. I'm here now so you can go back to what you were doing before this mess broke out."

"Okay," Libby said.

"Have you seen that man in her room before?" Ellie asked.

The nurse shifted on her feet and looked away. "Yes. He usually shows up when Dr. Rojas is in with her."

Ellie felt her body tremble. "How often?"

"Look, I don't want to lose my job."

"I promise you won't. Please tell me how often."

"When I've been here, maybe once a month."

"Thank you, Libby." Ellie tried to give the woman a reassuring smile. "Don't worry, your job is safe."

Libby nodded and left the room.

After checking that Syd was sleeping soundly and securely, Ellie pulled out her phone.

"Hey, how are you doing?"

"Jill, I need you to come here immediately."

"What's the matter," Jill said with an apprehensive voice.

"I found Syd. She's been here all along," Ellie whispered.

"Is she okay?"

"No. She has amnesia and some man has been doing something to her brain. I'm not sure what yet, but I'll find out."

"Tell me what you need."

"I need you to come here and stay with her so I can do some investigating."

"I'll throw some things together and leave immediately. Where will I find you?"

"Come to Salvation. I'll make sure the guards know you're coming. Get on the elevator and go to the fifth floor. It's room five twenty two."

"Okay. I'll see you soon."

After saying her goodbyes, Ellie called Syd's parents.

"Hi, I found Syd."

"Where? When? I can't believe it," Anita Tanner screamed. "Craig, Ellie's found Syd."

"Put that thing on speaker," Craig said. "Ellie, this is amazing. Where are you? We will come right away."

"No, don't do that yet."

"Why? Is she in trouble?" Anita asked.

"Not at the moment. She has amnesia and doesn't recognize me."

"Are you sure it's her?" Craig asked.

"If it isn't than this woman is a dead ringer for her down to that birthmark on her back. I'll get a cheek swab and compare it to the DNA results we got when she disappeared. They have a lab here where I can have the test done and I know a nurse who will do the swab for me."

"We can come get it. That might be faster," Craig said.

"Okay but first I need you to call Captain Barth and tell him that I found her and that it looks like they have been keeping her here without notifying the authorities. There was some man who came in her room and tried to hook her up to something that looked like some sort of shock therapy. I can't be sure but whatever it is I'd stake my medical license that it wasn't to do good."

"Oh, my God," Anita said. "My poor baby."

"To think we were there visiting you and she was so close by," Craig said. "I'll call Tom and let him know then we will be on our way."

"Can you tell him that I have the instrument that the man tried to use and I'm worried something will happen to it and me. These aren't nice people. Of that I'm sure."

"There's one sure way to keep that from happening," Anita said. "I'll call my friend at Channel Seven. They won't try much with reporters around."

"Great idea. Listen, there are things going on here that I need to look into before whoever is behind this comes around. Once I've established legally that this is indeed Syd—I know it's her—then I can use my power of attorney to get her out of here."

"Is she in danger, Ellie?"

"Not at the moment, Anita, but I am worried for her. I called Jill first so she could come right away and stay here with Syd. Now I need you to tell the captain and the news what is happening so we can stop any further harm to Syd. Once we straighten everything out, then we can all have a reunion with her."

"But she won't know us," Anita said sadly. "Will she ever?"

Ellie shook her head. "I don't know. I'll see you soon."

"We will be on our way. Craig is already on his phone speaking with Tom. I'll call my news friend from the car once we are on the road."

Ellie sighed. "Text me when you are within fifteen minutes and I'll make sure that the guards at the entrance know you're coming." She mentally shook her head. "Oh, she's in room five twenty two."

"Okay, darling, we will be there as fast as we can."

†

Ellie left the room and quickly found a swab for DNA and went back to Syd's room with Marie, the floor nurse, in tow. "I need you to swab the inside of her cheek and put the swab back in the container. Once that's done you need to initial it."

Marie carefully swabbed the sleeping woman's inner cheek and put the swab back in its plastic container.

"Anything else?" the nurse asked.

"Can you take that down to the lab and make sure it goes to Danny the lab tech. I've already spoken to him so he knows you're coming."

"Sure thing."

"Thanks, Marie." Once the door closed, Ellie rubbed her forehead and closed her eyes, hoping she hadn't made a mistake in trusting Marie or the lab tech. She wasn't worried since they could always do it again if necessary. Her phone vibrated—she had a text message from Anita. Pushing the screen she read…*Tom is going to escort us to where you are. He has already contacted the police there.*

Ellie smiled for it was as though they were reading her mind.

Syd moaned and Ellie was instantly bending over her wife. "Shhh, it's okay. You're safe."

After a long, deep yawn, Syd let out a sigh before her breathing evened and she was asleep again.

There was something niggling at her brain that she couldn't quite grasp. Ellie looked at the bag and knew it held the key to the mystery of Syd and what had happened to her. "I need to hide it someplace they won't find it until Captain Barth gets here." She looked around the room and saw no suitable hiding place. Her eyes widened. "I know just the place."

She quickly picked up the black bag, went to the door, opened it, and saw Libby coming out of a room. "Libby, are you busy?"

"I'm doing my rounds."

"Can you stay with this patient for about ten minutes? I'll clear it with Gretchen."

"Okay. Sure."

Ellie smiled and patted the woman's shoulder. "Thanks."

Once she made sure that Libby was covered on her rounds, Ellie took the black bag and made her way to the elevators—she needed to hide the bag.

After stepping out of the elevator, Ellie surveyed the area, making sure no one was there watching her. Across the atrium she saw the two guards. They glanced at her, then returned to their card game. With quick steps she went to her office, unlocked the door and after closing it, locked it behind her. At her desk she lifted the black bag and sat it on the surface. Putting on blue exam gloves she carefully began opening the case before looking at what was inside. There was a rectangular box that was about twelve inches by six with a half dozen leads coming out of the side. On the top there was some sort of screen that was blank. Ellie was tempted to turn the machine on but resisted for she didn't want to chance destroying evidence.

Instead she opened her desk drawer and picked up a small flat head screw driver. Closing the case and taking it with her she crouched down by the return air vent near the floor. Careful not to make any scratches or marks, she loosened the elaborate turn of the century grill and put the bag inside, pushing it back as far as possible before screwing the grill back on. Pleased with her work, she put the screwdriver back in the drawer and picked up her tablet before leaving the office.

In the atrium, she saw the two security guards still sitting where she noticed them before and went to them.

"In a couple hours a woman a little shorter than me with auburn hair will arrive. Check her ID to make sure her name is Jill Arnold. After that, show her to the elevators, okay?"

"Sure thing, Doc."

"Thanks." Ellie was about to go when she turned back to the men. "Tell me, that man that was here causing the trouble earlier... have you seen him here before?"

The two guards looked at one another and shrugged. Finally, the older one named Eddie spoke. "Yeah, he comes around about once a month."

"Is Dr. Rojas with him?"

They both shook their heads. "Not that I remember," Eddie said.

"How did he get in here tonight or any night for that matter."

"He shows up, gives us a pass and we let him in," said Marty, the younger man.

Eddie glared at his partner.

"A pass? What kind of pass? Do you have the one for tonight?"

"Sure do. Doc Rojas insists that we keep a log on who comes and goes at night," Tom said.

"May I see it?"

Eddie's eyes shifted and he torqued his jaw. "Um, sure, I guess you can...Doc gave us direct orders not to let them out of our sight."

"Well, I'm here tonight in place of Dr. Rojas so I'm sure it will be all right to let me see the card." Ellie fixed the man with a hard stare.

"Okay. I guess that makes you the boss." Eddie went to the desk and picked a card off the top of it. "Here you go."

Ellie's eyes scanned the card. It had Addison's name on it and was signed by none other than Maya Rojas. "You say you have records of all such cards."

"Not here with us. The doc takes all the visitor cards from us each morning."

"I see." Ellie held up the card she was holding. "Since I'm in charge I'll take this one with me."

"Um, not sure I can let you do that," Eddie said.

Ellie fixed him with a look that brooked no argument. "Yes, you can." She didn't wait for an answer and walked away. There was no way she would let this piece of information conveniently get lost. Maya Rojas was deep in whatever was being done to Syd and she wasn't going to let her continue. For a moment Ellie considered how she would get into Maya's office and search for the other visitor's cards then decided against it. *When the others get here I'll make sure they know about them. Right now I need to be with Syd.*

Chapter Nine

Ellie sat next to Syd's bed reading Jane's medical records on her tablet. The file showed that Syd came to Salvation a week after she disappeared. The patient—they called her Jane—had been at Salvation for six weeks before there was any record of the debilitating headaches. There was no mention of anyone contacting the authorities to notify them about a patient with amnesia.

Ellie found it curious that the part of the record where contact information for a next of kin was blank. *That should have been me.* She also noted that there wasn't any record of a Dr. Addison having any interaction with the patient. The only name that appeared as the attending physician was Dr. Maya Rojas. What also puzzled her was the indication that multiple scans had been done on Jane's brain yet she couldn't locate either the images or the reports.

A soft knock on the door drew Ellie's attention. "Jill." She stood and rushed into her sister's arms. "She doesn't know me," Ellie whispered.

Jill took a step back, released her sister, and moved to the bed. "She's thinner but that is definitely Syd."

Ellie managed a smile.

Syd's eyes flew open. "Who are you?" A terrified look passed between Jill and Ellie.

Jill reached down and ran her hand across Syd's forehead then down her cheek. "I'm Jill and I'm here for you."

For a long moment Syd stared at Jill then leaned into the hand that was still on her cheek before closing her eyes.

"You've always had that effect on her," Ellie said softly.

"Then maybe somewhere deep in her subconscious she remembers." Jill brushed Syd's cheek and smiled. "You found her and now we will work so she will remember us."

"We need to get her out of here, but first I need to make sure I have all the facts about what they've done to her so we can figure out a treatment plan."

"Sounds good. What do you want me to do?" Jill asked.

"I need to go to the cottage and get some of the documents that I'll need if I'm going to get her released from this place." She looked fondly at the woman in the bed. "You're the only one I trust to keep her safe while I'm not here." Ellie started for the door. "Oh, Craig and Anita are on their way with Captain Barth. If they get here before I get back, don't let them come in the room. It will be too much for her."

"You're probably right. Go ahead. I'll stay here and won't let anyone get near her." Jill touched Ellie's arm. "Once Terry takes the kids to his folks, he will come here too."

"I can't ask him to do that," Ellie said with tears in her eyes.

"He offered and said that you would need all the help you can get to get Syd back home." She pulled Ellie to her. "It's a good thing that the Tanners and the captain will be here. The more people the less underhanded whoever did this to Syd can be."

103

Ellie buried her head in her sister's shoulder. "I'm glad one of us is clear headed enough to think of all the things my brain is failing to recognize." She pulled away. "I'll text Craig on my way to the cottage and let him know not to come in here...we'll need to do that in stages. Are you okay here? You've got to be exhausted after driving for—" Ellie looked at her wrist watch. "How fast did you go? I only called you and hour and a half ago."

"Well...there was no traffic so I pushed the pedal to the floor on a few occasions." Jill grinned then gently pushed Ellie toward the door. "She's safe with me."

†

At the cottage Ellie grabbed the metal box that contained all the pertinent information to get Syd away from Salvation. She rifled through it and took out their marriage license and her power of attorney giving her the right to make decisions on Syd's behalf. A small picture on her dresser caught her attention and she removed the back of the frame and took out the picture. Having her ducks all in a row before Maya showed up—she had a feeling it would be sooner rather than later—was a must.

It had been fifteen minutes since she'd left Jill. At that point Ellie didn't know who she could trust at Salvation. If several of the staff ganged up on Jill she would be helpless. After looking around to make sure everything was as it should be, she hurried out the door.

†

Ellie was relieved to see Jill sitting by Syd's bed. "Hey, any trouble?"

"No. She woke up and looked at me and smiled. I take that as a sign that she knows we are here to help, not hurt."

"I agree." Ellie picked up her tablet. "I'm going to transfer all Syd's information to a cloud account I have. According to what I've gleaned so far they have been keeping her sedated most of the time. I did notice in the file that early on she did interact with other patients by playing scrabble." Ellie grinned. "She always beat me at that game."

Jill nodded. "I remember that."

Ellie took a deep breath and shook her head. "I can't believe no one here objected to her treatment...unless they are all in cahoots with whatever was being done to her."

"I don't believe that," Jill said before raising an eyebrow. "Won't they be able to trace where you send the files?"

"Probably but I have it set up so that any file I put in there is automatically backed up on a hard drive at my house. By the time they find that it will be too late for them."

"Does the captain have jurisdiction here?"

"No, but Craig said he's already been in touch with the local police. I need to speak with Maya and see if she is willing to share her involvement into what was happening to Syd. It seems like she was in the thick of things."

"Why bother? You know she was involved, don't you? We have Syd. Let's take her away from here right now."

"Not until I find out what they've done to her. We can't treat her unless we know the whole story on how she came to be here and why that man was using that machine."

"Why not let the police handle that, Ellie. That's their job, not yours."

Ellie looked at Syd and smiled before fixing her eyes on Jill. "Because they won't know the right questions to ask."

"Come on, they aren't stupid."

"They don't love Syd...."

The door burst open and an angry Maya was standing in the doorway. "What the hell have you done?"

Ellie looked at Maya. "Shall we take this to my office?"

Red-faced, Maya turned and walked away.

"Don't let anyone come near her. I'll be back." Ellie touched Jill's hand. "Craig texted me and said they were about twenty minutes out. Will you be okay until they get here?"

Jill nodded. "No one will get to her, I promise."

"I know. Thanks."

"It might be a good idea to inform reporters too."

"Anita has already taken care of that. Finding Syd is big news and that will work to our advantage."

†

When Ellie got to her office door, Maya was standing there tapping her foot with a sneer on her face.

Ellie only shook her head and unlocked the door, motioning for Maya to go inside. *There's no way I'll turn my back on her.* She knew once she revealed exactly who *Jane* was and their connection she would have the upper hand.

Once in the office Maya turned toward Ellie with an angry expression. "Do you have any idea how much damage you've done to Salvation?"

Ellie fixed Maya with a glare. "You had an amnesia patient in this facility that you didn't bother to find an identity for."

"That's not true," Maya countered. "We alerted the police and they came up with nothing."

"Liar!" Ellie screamed. She pulled the picture of Syd from her pocket and shoved it in Maya's face. "This is my wife, Syd Tanner. Recognize her? She's been missing for seven months. There was a nationwide hunt for her. It was in all the news reports. If you'd reported her, then I would have come and claimed her so don't give me all your bullshit about trying to identify her!"

Maya eyes widened before lowering her head and shaking it. "They gave me no choice."

"You always have a choice and yours was to let that man use my wife as an experiment."

"They would have killed her if I didn't comply," Maya whispered.

"You're kidding, right? That man was killing her brain and you allowed it to happen, Maya. You let her be tortured!"

"I made sure that she wasn't all the way out so he couldn't do it most of the time."

"How many times did you let that evil man do that to her?"

"Six or seven before you came. After you suggested another treatment plan, she was never so bad that he could do anything."

"How did he know to come tonight?"

Maya shook her head. "I don't know how he knows. I've suspected someone on the floor tells him but I've never been able to find a common denominator among the staff."

"God, I can't believe this. Or you. What happened to *first do no harm*? You really had me going there, thinking you were such a wonderful compassionate person. One who I was beginning to care for." Ellie snorted. "How wrong for me to think that." She pulled out the power of attorney. "This is a copy of a power of attorney that I have regarding Syd and her care, should she become incapacitated. As soon as Syd's parents and the police captain in charge of Syd's case arrive we will be taking her out of this hell hole and charging you along with that so called Dr. Addison with kidnapping."

"You can't do that! You don't have any proof."

Ellie laughed. "Oh, but I have more than enough proof to sink you and him. Did you really think once I found Syd that I would just sit back and do nothing?"

"By telling others, you've made the situation a hundred times worse. These people are powerful with connections everywhere. Do you think they will just sit by and let you take her?" Maya snorted. "If you do then you are delusional."

"You really thought I'd keep quiet and not tell anyone? I had your pal Addison arrested for assault and the police back in Clifton Heights are on their way here as we speak." Ellie looked at her watch. "They should be arriving at any minute." She fixed her gaze on Maya. "You kidnapped her and kept her drugged so your pal could experiment on her. How could you do that to another human being?"

"I did not harm her—they did."

"But you stood by and let it happen to one of *your* patients."

"Didn't you sign an admittance form earlier today for someone that you didn't even examine?" Maya asked definitely. "I can play the game too, Elinor. If you try to involve me then that admittance form you signed will be the end of your career."

Ellie laughed. "I'm not stupid. Your pal Addison was in such a hurry he didn't bother to check the form out. If you look at it you will see that I added *under duress* below my name. Don't for one minute think I won't tell them about the patients that get admitted by you that never show up as being here. I'm surprised that you actually had Syd's records."

Maya's eyes widened. "You have those? They are confidential. You can't have them."

"As medical director, I have full access to everything. A crime has been committed and those records are evidence of that crime. There's no way I'm going to let you, or Addison, off the hook."

For a long while Maya stared at Ellie. "They would have kicked me to the curb and made sure I'd never practice medicine again if I didn't cooperate."

"And that was reason enough to compromise your principles?" Ellie sneered at the woman who was now a stranger to her. "That's just sick."

"Do you really think they will not come after Jane just because you move her?"

"Syd, her name is Dr. Sydney Tanner. Let them try to get to her. I promise you that I will *never* let that happen. As we speak every news outlet is being alerted to finding her at Salvation held as a prisoner against her will after you kidnapped her." Ellie sighed. "I was wrong about you and now you and Addison and whoever else is involved is going down."

Maya blew out a breath and shook her head. "I had no involvement in her abduction. The first I knew about her was when Addison showed up with her one rainy night. You have no idea who you're dealing with and the power they have."

"Bring it on. They have no idea what I am capable of when it comes to protecting my wife."

"They have my brother," Maya whispered.

Ellie snorted. "I'm not falling for that. If they have him—if you even have a brother—that would have been the first excuse you'd give me." She narrowed her eyes. "Face it. You've played and lost."

The sound of sirens filled the night air.

"Time's up, Doctor, and you haven't given me any reason to protect you from what is about to happen. I really thought…"

She shrugged. "It doesn't matter now what I thought, for you never were that person."

Ellie went to the door and opened it. When she saw Captain Barth along with other police officers she motioned them into her office.

"Captain Barth, it's good to see you. This is Dr. Maya Rojas, who is the director of this facility and has been treating Sydney Tanner for the past six to seven months." Ellie looked at Maya and sighed.

A tall muscular woman dressed in jeans, a white shirt, and blazer stepped forward. "Dr. Rojas, I'm Detective Rachel Lambert from the Overton police department. I need you to come with me to the station and answer some questions related to Dr. Sydney Tanner and her disappearance."

"I know nothing of this Dr. Tanner. Jane's husband admitted her because she became delusional."

"And her name just happened to be Jane Doe?" Ellie let out a sarcastic laugh.

"That is the name he gave me."

Rachel Lambert took Maya's arm. "Please, Dr. Rojas, come with me."

"Fine. Am I being arrested?"

"No, ma'am, we just want to question you."

"I want my lawyer present."

"That is your right. We can make the call on our way."

Maya glared at Ellie before nodding at the other woman.

"Are you coming, Captain?" the detective asked.

"Yes, right behind you."

Captain Barth was about to follow before Ellie gripped his arm.

"I'd like to sit in on that interview," he said.

"I know, I just need a minute of your time."

"Detective Lambert, I'll be with you in a minute."

Once everyone was gone, Ellie moved to her desk and took out the screwdriver. "I have something to give you. I don't know the others but I know you and this is too valuable to lose." She put on exam gloves before proceeding to the vent, taking the cover off, and pulling out the black bag. "This is the instrument that the man was trying to use on Syd."

The captain took a glove out of his pocket and took the bag. "What is it?"

"I don't know but I suspect they were using it to do some sort of mind control."

"I'll lock it in my trunk and once we've interviewed Dr. Rojas and that Addison fellow, I'll make sure it is secured so no one else will have access to it."

"Thank you," Ellie said. "Oh, and I also have all the records of the treatment they were giving Syd. There is no mention of anyone being next of kin and Dr. Rojas is the only name on the records."

"Doesn't that go to doctor patient confidentiality?"

Ellie held up her power of attorney. "This supersedes that."

The captain patted Ellie's arm. "I won't let them get away with this you have my word on that."

"Thank you."

†

Ellie stepped outside her door and Craig and Anita ran toward her before engulfing her in a fierce hug.

"Can I see her," Anita cried.

Ellie felt her body relax as she sank into their hugs. "Sure. Just remember she won't know you and may be afraid when she sees you."

"I don't care. She's my baby and I need to see her."

"Come on then. Jill is with her."

"Thank God you found her," Anita whispered. "I can't believe she was here all the time."

"Me either." Ellie put her arm around Anita's shoulder as she led her to her daughter.

Chapter Ten

Jane opened her eyes and looked at the woman sitting in a chair next to the bed reading. Initially she was terrified when the stranger came in her room but that was momentary. The minute the woman—she thought her name was Jill— came to her and smoothed her hand over her face, a strange sensation suffused her, causing her to relax into the caress. She closed her eyes and a vision of the doctor who stood up to the white haired man by placing herself in a protective position filled her mind's eye. For the first time since arriving at Salvation, she felt safe.

They both said they knew her and that her name was Sue...no, Syd. That's what the doctor said. *Syd.* She let the name roll around in her head for several minutes but in the end it wasn't familiar. The only name she knew was Jane— anything else was foreign to her. But at least someone knew her and had found her there. The fact that they were willing to be her protectors was more than a bonus.

Her mind wandered back to when she had arrived at Salvation. She recalled waking up and wondering where she was, unable to remember how she got there. As hard as Jane tried, she couldn't remember anything After that, she was in a drugged haze most of the time. She started cheeking her pills, then throwing them away. It was then that the headaches started and Dr. Rojas started giving her injections and allowing the white haired man to come and torture her.

It wasn't until the other doctor—*her last name was Scott, I think*—said she knew her. Up until that moment she didn't have any hope of finding her memories. Had she finally turned the corner and would no longer be in the fog that had invaded her mind since she woke up in this place? *God, I hope so.* There was a slight rap on the door and Jane opened her eyes in terror. "Don't let them hurt me," she cried.

Jill was immediately by Syd's side. "I won't let anyone hurt you. Let me see who it is."

†

When the door opened and Anita saw Jill she craned her neck to get a glimpse of her daughter. "I have to see her."

Jill smiled at the couple and Ellie. "Just one at a time. Right now she is very skittish, so don't rush to her even though you want to."

"It will be hard but I won't...I promise."

The door opened wider and Anita walked slowly toward the bed where her daughter's familiar hazel eyes stared at her. "Hi, how are you doing, sweetheart," she said in her most soothing mother's voice.

Jane pulled the sheet up and bunched it near her neck. "Do I know you?" Jane asked with a tremulous voice.

"Yes." Anita looked at Ellie and when she nodded, she smiled. "I'm your mother."

"I have a mother?" Jane's eyes darted to Jill, who closed her eyes then opened them.

"Yes," Jill whispered.

"That's who I am." Anita resisted the urge to reach out and touch her daughter. "And you have a father, too. Would you like to meet him?"

"I...I don't know." Jane held her head. "This is all too much for me."

"It's okay, darling. We can wait until you're comfortable around me before you meet him," Anita soothed. She reached out and gently brushed her fingers along her daughter's cheek.

Jane's eyes widened and she moved away from the touch before reconsidering and leaning into it and closing her eyes.

Ellie watched the unravelling scene and she felt hope for Syd's memory return. She walked to the bed and smiled down at her wife. "Are you doing okay? Do you need anything?"

Jane began shivering and her face turned ashen. "What's happening to me? I feel so strange." Her eyes rolled back and she started to convulse.

Ellie pushed the chair away from the bed, made sure the sheet and gown were not constricting the airway, and gently turned Syd on her side. "Anita, get close to the bottom of the bed to stop her if she begins to roll out."

The seizure lasted forty-five seconds and when it ended. Syd looked dazed and disoriented.

"You're okay," Ellie said. "Just rest and take in some deep breaths. We'll be here for you. You're safe."

"Wh...what happened?"

With a gentle touch Ellie moved her lover's hair out of her eyes. "You had a seizure. Have you had them before?"

"No," Jane whispered weakly.

Ellie stroked the black hair and smiled down at her wife. "It's okay. Rest now." Her fingers continued to caress the locks of hair as Syd closed her eyes and her breath evened out. Ellie leaned in and placed a gentle kiss on her head before standing.

"Is she going to be okay?" Anita asked.

"Until I can determine exactly what's been done to her, I just don't know. I'm hoping it is something that can be reversed, but I have no idea if that is even possible. There is every likelihood that she will never regain her memory." Ellie blew out a breath.

Anita's hand covered her mouth. "Oh, my God, no."

Ellie pulled Anita into her arms. "I'm not giving up hope that she will return to us just as she was before she went missing." She took a step back. "I don't believe in coincidences. Providence brought me here to find Syd and it will lead her back to us."

"You truly believe that?"

"Yes. Yes, I do."

Both women turned to see Craig and Jill standing in the doorway.

"We need to get her out of here and I'm not sure how to go about that," Ellie said. "The power of attorney I have should be enough but it is obvious we are going against something evil."

"Do you want me to call my attorney?" Craig asked.

Ellie considered his words for a few seconds. "Yes. We need to know we are on solid legal ground." She smiled at Craig. "When she wakes up, she won't know you and will probably be frightened. Why don't you sit beside her and spend a few moments with her then we can go to my office and sort things out."

"Thank you." Craig moved close to the bed and bent to kiss Syd's cheek. "She's so thin," he whispered as he sat next to the bed. "Hi, baby, I know you don't know who I am but know that I, along with everyone who loves you, will keep you safe." He kissed her again then stood. "Let's get things rolling."

Ellie nodded. "Anita, will you and Jill stay with her?" She looked at her watch. "They should be serving breakfast soon."

A sudden chill ran down her spine. "Jill, will you go to the cottage and make some toast and eggs and bring them back for her. Something tells me not to trust the food they bring her."

"On it," Jill said. "Anita, I'll be gone for about a half hour max. Will you be okay here alone?"

Anita snorted. "Let them try to come near her. They'll find a mama bear guarding her young."

"Okay, mama bear," Craig said before he kissed his wife. "If you need anything, just call and I'll be here in a flash."

†

Ellie unlocked her office door and she and Craig walked inside before closing the door behind them. "Go ahead and use my desk and phone. The sooner we know where we stand legally, the sooner we can get Syd out of here."

"From what you've told me, I don't think it will be wise to use your phone," Craig said as he sat down. "I'll use my cell. I think it will be safer."

"You're absolutely correct." Ellie shook her head. "I don't know what I was thinking."

"Have you had any sleep?"

The warm, fatherly voice warmed Ellie. "Not since—" she looked at her wrist watch. "I got up yesterday morning."

117

"Why don't you stretch out on that couch while I make my call."

"I can't. There's too much I need to do before whoever is behind this rallies the troops and comes after Syd."

"You won't do anyone any good if you're exhausted. Why don't you get an hour's sleep, then we will tackle this problem together."

"Promise you won't let me sleep too long?"

"I promise. Now go lay down."

Ellie was too exhausted to argue but she was so wound up that she didn't think she could sleep. "Okay." She moved to the couch and sat.

Just then there was a rap on the door before it opened. In walked four suits—one woman and three men.

"Dr. Scott?" the woman asked.

Ellie stood. "Who's asking?"

"I'm Dr. Miranda English," she pointed to the man next to her, "This is Dr. Herman Bolger and next to him are Edgar Vincent and Dr. Vladimir Rumski. We are on the board of directors for Salvation." She looked at Craig sitting at the desk with his phone to his ear. "You may leave."

"No. He stays." Ellie glared at the woman who was wearing a black suit with a red silk shirt. "From what I've seen so far, I wouldn't be alone with any of you."

"Now, now, Dr. Scott, please don't judge us by how others have acted. I assure you we are only interested in what is best for Salvation."

"Yeah, right. You've allowed someone to be kept here against her will without notifying the authorities of her existence."

"That is not something we are aware of," Dr. English said in a cool tone.

Ellie just shook her head and looked at Craig who still had his phone in his hand. *Good, our lawyer is hearing all of this. Let's see if I can use it to my advantage.* "I find that hard to believe, Dr. English. I was told by Dr. Rojas that the board had an active hand in the running of Salvation. You being here suggests that is a true statement and I can only deduce that you are aware of all the irregularities going on here."

Dr. Rumski, who had thick bushy eyebrows and a craggy face moved forward. "Just what are you accusing us of, Dr. Scott," he said in a thickly accented voice.

"The list is endless, Dr. Rumski. Once the police finish their investigation, it will all come out."

Miranda English pushed the man aside and walked to within a foot of Ellie. "We will void your contract and pay you three years' salary as compensation."

"In return for what?"

"You leave and take the press and police with you."

"Hmm, that sounds like a bribe," she looked at Craig. "Does it to you, too, Dad?"

"That's what it sounds like to me," Craig answered.

Rumski was in Ellie's face. "How dare you insinuate that we would stoop to such measures. You don't fit here, Doctor, and we are being generous with you." He pointed a gnarled finger in her direction. "How dare you accuse us of something so underhanded."

Dr. English's hand was on the man's shoulder. "Vlad, let me handle this." Her voice was low and held a hint of command. "Why don't you and the others wait outside for me."

Ellie recognized an order when she heard it. *So, Dr. English, you are the one in charge. Interesting.* She watched as the men left the room.

"Will you please ask him to leave," she nodded in Craig's direction. "So we can speak privately?"

"No, I don't think so."

Craig lowered his phone and placed it on the desk. "It's okay, Ellie. I'll be right outside if you need me."

"I don't feel safe." Ellie watched Craig's eyes glance quickly toward his phone. "You'll come if I call?"

"In a heartbeat."

Ellie nodded and Craig left the room.

"You have nothing to fear from me, Doctor," the woman purred. "Just like you I want to get to the bottom of this."

"Really?"

"Please," she pointed to the couch. "Sit and let's see if we can come to some sort of agreement about this predicament we both find ourselves in."

Ellie reluctantly sat. "I doubt seriously that there is anything you can tell me, Dr. English, that will dissuade me from doing what I must."

"What is it you feel you must do, Elinor?"

She's used my first name. Fascinating. So this is the game she wants to play. Even though she was running on fumes Ellie rose to the occasion. "Other than the bribe, what are you thinking of doing?"

Miranda visibly bristled. "That was not a bribe. Your present contract is for three years. When we decide to let someone go it is standard practice to buy out the rest of the contract."

"Really? I don't recalling reading anything like that in the contract I signed." Ellie shrugged. "Nor do I recall Dr. Rojas ever mentioning such a thing. I'd think that would be a selling point to get someone to sign the contract."

"Look, what has happened here is unconscionable, but it has happened and now we need to make it right. Please don't put all your emphasis on Salvation as a whole. We are not the bad guys. We obviously had some rogue employees that have tarnished our good name, but I assure you that is not who I or the other board members are. We want only the best for those who come to us for help."

"Are you for real?" Ellie asked. "Are you telling that those who have a vested interest in Salvation don't have some sort of oversight committee?" She sneered at the woman. "Do you really think I am that clueless?"

Miranda touched Ellie's arm.

Ellie pulled her arm away and moved farther down the coach.

"Don't you dare touch me," she said. "I am taking the patient that is listed as Jane Doe out of this place and I'll take the severance pay for it will take all of that and more to help her get her memory back."

"If I agree, then you will let this go?"

Ellie shook her head. She couldn't remember when she'd been this weary. "After what has happened here to my wife there is no way I'll ever let this go." She dragged her fingers through her hair. "Frankly, I don't know if you are involved or not." She shrugged. "But someone violated Syd in an reprehensible way and it happened here at this facility. Ultimately, Dr. English, you and your board are responsible."

"Then I cannot let you take Jane from here."

"That is where you are wrong, *Miranda*. You don't mind if I call you by your first name, do you?" Ellie watched the woman's eyes widen. "As I was saying, I have the legal right to take her with me."

Miranda smiled. "You have to prove she is who you say she is and I'll bar you and all those with you from Salvation."

"Is that a threat, Dr. English?"

"No. It is a promise. I didn't get where I am by not knowing how to play hard ball."

Ellie stood, walked to the desk, picked up the phone, and held it to her ear. "Did you hear all that?" She pressed the speaker button.

"Yes, I did and my paralegal is with me taking notes."

"That is the voice of Edward Sims who is my lawyer." Ellie smiled. "I know how to play hard ball too, especially when it involves my family."

"Dr. Scott, your power of attorney, along with the medical power of attorney, gives you the right to take Dr. Tanner from Salvation at any time you please," the lawyer interjected.

Ellie felt the ice in her veins as she glared at Miranda English. "Thank you, Ed, please stay on the line."

"Will do."

"Have all the medical records you have pertaining to the patient known as Jane Doe ready by—" Ellie looked at her wrist watch. "Noon. She will be leaving this facility at that time. I'll request that the police be present to ensure nothing happens when we leave. In the meantime, she is being cared for by family who will protect her with their lives."

"There is no need to involve the police, Dr. Scott. You will have all the records but we will have to insist on an exit examination."

Ellie laughed. "Not on your life will I let anyone connected with Salvation to get near her. I am her physician of record and I alone will examine her and pronounce her fit to leave this place."

"It is our policy that one of our doctors examine the patient. That is non-negotiable," Miranda said in a voice full of bravado.

"The last I looked, Miranda, I am a member of the staff here and a medical doctor, so cut the bullshit. I've had enough."

"You're fired," Miranda countered. "Therefore you are not on the staff."

"Ed, am I obligated to let them examine her?"

"No. You have the right to make all medical decisions for Syd."

"There. You have your answer."

"You will need to sign that she is leaving against doctor's orders," Miranda countered.

"Look, Miranda, don't make this worse than it already is. Right now you and this facility are in hot water, not only with the police and the suit I am going to bring against Salvation and its board, but the news people who are camped outside."

Ellie closed her eyes attempting to tamp down the rage she was feeling. "Please leave so I can clear out this office and arrange for movers to pack my things in the cottage."

"We have lawyers too."

"Of course you do. I'll make sure you have my lawyer's information. Now, please leave."

Miranda straightened her shoulders and walked to the door. "You have no idea what you've done," she whispered.

"Nor do you." Ellie watched the door close behind the woman before she picked up the phone on the desk. "Thank you, Ed. Am I on solid ground here?"

"Yes.

"Thank you. I'll be in touch." Ellie ended the call just as the door opened and Craig walked in.

"Everything okay here?"

"Yes." Ellie's shoulders fell and she began to cry.

Craig gathered his daughter-in-law into his arms. "Let it all go. I've got you."

†

As quietly as possible, Ellie opened the door to Syd's room. She saw Anita lying next to her daughter with her arm wrapped protectively around her—both sleeping. Jill sat with her feet elevated in one of those uncomfortable faded green recliners that hospitals always seemed to have. She was sleeping.

Seeing the sight reminded Ellie again about how exhausted she was. There was so much left to do before she could get Syd out of Salvation and back home where she belonged. After several unsuccessful attempts, she was able to find a mover that would pack her belongings the next day which was a relief. That of course meant Syd had to remain at Salvation for another day and night. The idea didn't make Ellie happy but she knew that with the support that surrounded her, Syd would be safe.

Jill opened her eyes. "Hey, how is everything going?" She got up and went to Ellie who was standing in the doorway. "Let's go outside so we don't wake them."

Ellie nodded and they left the room, closing the door softly behind them. "I've given Captain Barth the bag I took from Addison, gave the police a statement, found movers, and had four members of Salvation's Board of Directors visit me." She let a weary smile wreath her lips. "Everything is coming together and we can get Syd out of here tomorrow."

"Why not today?"

"I won't leave until all my things are packed and gone. There's no way I'll trust anyone here not to ransack the cottage or my office." Ellie closed her eyes. "I'm so tired but I can't let my guard down."

"I've slept. Why don't you let me take over for you and you get some rest." Jill put her arm around her sister's shoulders. "Come on. That recliner isn't so bad and you will be in the room with Syd."

"I've got to clear out my office."

Jill held out her hand. "Keys." When Ellie didn't respond she shook her hand. "Come on give me the keys to your office and cottage. I know what belongs to you and what doesn't. Please let me do this for you."

"But—"

"No buts. You're sluggish and won't be fit to do anything when the time comes to leave here. Right now you need to sleep."

"Okay, but just for an hour or so. I've done stressful forty-eight hour rotations, this, in comparison, is a piece of cake." Ellie reached in her pocket and handed the keys over to Jill.

"Right. Now let's get you settled and I'll go to the cottage freshen up and come back with boxes for your office things."

"Don't let me sleep too long," Ellie said as she sank into the chair.

"Sleep. I'll be back soon."

†

Ellie woke with a start and looked around the hospital room. Anita was gone and Syd was lying in her bed staring at the ceiling. With a practiced gaze Ellie watched for the rise and fall of Syd's chest—she was breathing.

"Good morning. How are you feeling?" Ellie asked.

Jane turned her head and her forehead furrowed. "My head hurts."

"Do you want me to get your something to ease the pain?" Ellie lowered the foot rest and stood.

"No drugs," Jane whispered. "Bad things happen then."

"I won't let that happen." Ellie cautiously moved toward the bed. "Tomorrow I'll take you out of this place to somewhere where you will be safe and no one can hurt you again."

Dull eyes began to tear. "You can't promise that."

Ellie knelt by the bed and ran her fingers across the furrowed brow. "Yes. Yes, I can. I won't let anything bad happen to you ever again. That's a promise and I always keep my promises."

Jane moved away from the touch and pressed the button so the back of the bed elevated. She grimaced.

"Tell me where the pain is."

"Here." Jane touched the right side of her head.

"Is it a stabbing pain or a dull ache."

"Most of the time it is a constant ache but at least once a day it is like a hot poker is stabbing inside my head."

"Are the times when that happen the same?"

Jane looked at the ceiling. "Usually after dinner time."

Ellie saw Syd's intelligent eyes come to life. *There's hope. I can see it in her eyes.* "Was it after that they gave you your medications?"

"Yes. I pretended to take them and spit it out once they left. It was after that the pain began and Dr. Rojas started giving me injections."

Ellie was furious by what she'd heard. It was obvious that they were inducing the pain and she wondered if it was so Addison could come and do whatever it was he did to her. "Never again," she growled. "I won't allow anyone to abuse you like that again."

"Why do you care? No one else has."

Ellie saw a marked difference from the night before. There was a feistiness—one that she'd always associated with Syd—coming back to life. "No one has given you any medication this morning, have they?"

"No. A nurse came in, saying it was time for my meds but those two women wouldn't let her give them to me. Especially the older one. She got right up in the nurse's face and told her to get out."

A genuine smile crossed Ellie's face. "A lioness protecting her cub," she said. "Your mother has always been a force to reckon with when it came to you."

"She's really my mother," Jane whispered.

"Yes."

"Who are you to me?"

Ellie considered her answer. She didn't want to cause information overload but at the same time truth was what she knew in her heart was right. "I'm your wife."

Jane's eyes widened and her mouth opened only to close again. "We're married," she said finally.

"Yes. For almost ten years." Ellie held her breath, hoping for anything but a negative reaction.

Jane rubbed her head. "I don't remember." She looked at Ellie. "What happened to me?"

"I don't know. One night you didn't come home. I searched for you everywhere but you had vanished and we couldn't find you."

With tears streaming down her cheeks, Jane held her head with both hands. "I don't know you. I'm sorry."

Ellie sat on the side of the bed and pulled the woman she knew to be Syd into her arms and cried with her. "Return to me, Syd," she whispered into the black hair.

The door opened and Anita walked into the room. "I've brought you both lunch."

"You didn't get it from here did you?" Ellie asked.

"No, darling, I made it myself." Anita looked at her daughter and smiled. "I made your favorite. Grilled cheese and tomato soup."

Ellie pulled away but stayed sitting on the bed.

Jane took the offered sandwich and took a bite and let out a satisfied sigh. "I don't remember this being my favorite but it is very good."

"You will in time, sweetheart." Anita ran a hand through the long hair. "I promise you that."

Jane put the sandwich down and shook her head. "You can't promise that...neither of you can. I don't remember anything before I came here."

Anita only smiled. "I have faith and it has never let me down."

Chapter Eleven

It wasn't until Monday that they were able to bring Syd back to Clifton Heights. The board members tried another legal maneuver to keep her there but Ellie would have none of it and in the end she got her way. They still paid her three year's salary—they said it was to show their good faith and willingness to cooperate in any way possible. Ellie scoffed at Dr. English's thinly vailed threat that she keep her mouth shut now that they'd paid her off. Fat chance of that happening.

Jill and Terry left two days earlier so they would be there when the movers arrived and make sure everything at the house was as it should be. They also moved all of Syd's clothes and belongings to the guest bedroom. The last thing Ellie wanted to do was make her wife feel uncomfortable.

During the days that Anita spent with her daughter, they formed a bond and that gave them all encouragement for Syd's full recovery. Unfortunately, Syd chose to ride back to Clifton Heights with Anita, leaving Ellie to follow behind. Her heart ached. Next to losing Syd seven months earlier, this was the hardest thing she'd ever had to do. Being so close to Syd and not able to run her fingers through her hair or kiss her was killing her. As long as she knew Syd was safe, Ellie was willing to be patient and take as long as needed for Syd to return to who she was. If that didn't happen, then Ellie's hope was that they would fall in love all over again.

†

She'd been there a week and Jane once again wandered through the house that her mother said she had lived in with the woman doctor. It was obvious, by looking at all the pictures, that she and Ellie had been a couple. As she looked around, she touched everything hoping that something would spark a memory that would open the door to her past. Nothing did and she was beginning to wonder if she'd ever go back to being someone named Syd Tanner.

She picked up a picture that depicted a wedding—her wedding. The women in the picture were smiling broadly while looking into one another's eyes. Their joy was evident as was the love they obviously felt for one another. Jane had seen the same look in the doctor's eyes every time their eyes met.

"Why can't I feel anything? Their love is so obvious you'd think it would be something I'd never forget," she muttered. She felt her heart deflating from the frustration at what should have been familiar yet wasn't and she had no hope that it would ever return. A stab of pain shot through the side of her head and she let out a cry as she clasped her head in her hand.

The doctor was by her side instantly. "Here," she said, taking Syd's arm, "let me help you."

Jane's natural instinct was to pull away but the pain was so intense that she melted into the touch and allowed the doctor to guide her to the couch. Once seated she cradled her head and cried out. "Make the pain stop. Please, take it away."

"Slow your breathing down," Ellie said softly. "Breathe in through your nose and blow out through your mouth."

"What good will that do?"

"You can try that or I can give you drugs. The choice is yours."

"No drugs." Jane followed the instructions concentrating on her breathing and soon she felt her body begin to relax. It didn't take long for her to yawn. "It's letting up," she whispered.

"Good. Keep concentrating on your breathing. That's it, nice and easy."

The doctor's hand lightly massaging the base of her neck caused Jane to lean into it while her body completely relaxed. She opened her eyes then closed them, relishing the feeling of being relatively pain free and safe. *She makes me feel safe and cared for.* Jane couldn't remember a time since her ordeal began that anyone made her feel that way. *Not even Dr. Rojas did that.* Suddenly aware of the doctor's proximity to her, Jane pulled away. "Thank you. I feel much better now."

Ellie smiled and moved away. "Why don't you go lay down and see if you can nap. These episodes always zap your energy. If you can't sleep, then just rest."

"I think I'll do that." Jane looked at the doctor and once again saw the sorrow in her eyes. "The next time it happens, I'll try to remember to slow my breathing and relax."

"When pain grabs us, like it just did you, our body tenses and that makes the pain more intense."

"So I should go with the flow?"

"Exactly. It won't stop the pain but it will make it more manageable."

"Thank you, Doctor." Jane saw the woman flinch at her words.

Ellie patted her hand and nodded. "Go on and get some rest. I'm going to see about making dinner."

"Okay." Jane stood and walked toward her room before stopping and turning around. "I'm sorry. I wish I could remember. Thank you for everything, Ellie."

†

Ellie blew out a breath. That was the closest that Syd—*no, Jane*—had let her get and it was all she could do to squelch her desire.

I must remember that she is now Jane and doesn't remember our life together, much less our love for one another.

"Easier said than done."

When she had massaged Jane's neck, she'd felt her lean into the touch. "I wonder if she felt anything?" *Probably not, but maybe…*

When they'd first met, it was instant attraction for them both. Ellie smiled, remembering their first date at a hole in the wall restaurant that Syd said served 'out of this world' hamburgers—and they were.

"I wonder if that place is still in business? Easy way to find out." Ellie pulled out her phone and Googled Archie's Hideaway. "Yes!"

She smiled. "If she fell in love with me before as Syd, the chances are good that Jane will fall in love with me, too. Our chemistry has always been intense."

She high-fived the air before heading for the kitchen and salmon that was waiting to be cooked.

†

Jane woke with a start. The depression and lingering discomfort she would usually feel after a bout of severe pain was not there. Instead a sense of peace enveloped her body, making her feel warm and safe. She gingerly sat upright expecting to feel the searing pain. Nothing. "That's a relief. This has never happened before and all it took was deep breathing and no drugs."

She walked to the dresser and peered at herself in the mirror, trying to reconcile the woman in the pictures with the one she saw. They looked the same although Jane noticed she was thinner than the Syd person but they were essentially the same. "Who are you?" As with every time she asked the question the answer was the same. "Jane."

Opening the door, her nose was immediately drawn to the delightful smells that were filling the area. *I wonder what she's cooking tonight.* Her mouth watered. Every meal she'd had since arriving there had been outstanding and nothing like what she'd had at Salvation. With a spring in her step, she followed her nose.

†

The doctor was in the kitchen preparing dinner and Jane stood in the entryway watching her. She was humming to a tune that was coming from somewhere as she danced in place. Jane's eyes roamed across the swaying hips before looking at the doctor's face. There was no doubt that the doctor was a beautiful woman and Jane reflected on the kindness the woman had always shown her.

"I wish I could remember you," she whispered.

The doctor turned as if she'd heard and smiled. "How are you feeling?"

"Good. There is the dull ache I always feel, but the intensity is gone. Thank you for helping me, Ellie." A genuine smile curved the full lips and Jane was happy she was responsible for that.

"I hope you still like salmon," Ellie said.

"I don't remember ever having it." Jane frowned. "Everything you make is delicious, so I am sure I'll like salmon." She stepped farther into the kitchen. "Do you need any help?"

"Sure. That would be great. Will you make a salad?'

"Sure." Jane had to look away—the doctor's haunted blue eyes held so much meaning that it put Jane into sensory overload. She went to the refrigerator and pulled out Romaine lettuce, cherry tomatoes, and a cucumber. After rinsing the lettuce she began to pull it apart in small pieces placing them in a wooden salad bowl she took out of a cupboard. Once the salad ingredients were mixed, she took out bottles of balsamic vinegar and olive oil along with garlic and a variety of spices.

Ellie watched in amazement as Jane prepared what she had called her specialty salad complete with her secret recipe dressing. She used all the same utensils and seemed to know where everything was. For the first time since that awful night that Syd disappeared, Ellie had a sense of real optimism.

"I hope you're hungry. It looks like I've made enough for an army." Ellie looked at the plates filled with fish, roasted Brussel sprouts, and rice pilaf.

"It smells wonderful and I must admit I am hungry." Jane cocked her head. "I never remember ever feeling hungry at Salvation." She shrugged. "The food wasn't that good."

Ellie felt a shiver go up her spine when she heard the word *Salvation*. Never again would those evil doers get their hands on her wife. If she ever saw Maya Rojas or Spencer Addison again, they would be sorry. She looked at Jane and smiled. "Are you ready for the feast I've prepared."

"My mouth has been watering since I smelled it cooking so I am ready, Freddy."

Ellie's heart lurched. *Ready Freddy* was a term Syd always used. "Put your salad on the table and I'll bring in the rest."

Jane smiled and picked up the salad bowl after fishing the wooden spoons that went with the bowl out of the drawer.

As long as it takes, I'll be with you all the way, my love.

Ellie picked up the plates and followed the gently moving hips into the dining room.

†

"This is delicious," Jane said putting her fork down.

"Thank you. I'm glad you like it. Cooking is one of my favorite things to do." Ellie smiled at her.

Jane looked away, her mind jumbled with so many questions she didn't know where to start. When she looked at Ellie again she took in a deep breath. "Did I cook too?"

A warm smile curved Ellie's lips. "Yes," she said. "We had different shifts with our jobs so when we were here together at meal time, we'd make dinner together." Ellie tapped the salad bowl. "This salad was your specialty. You had a unique recipe for the dressing that was outstanding."

Jane was confused. "I made this salad before? I don't remember."

Again Ellie smiled. "Yes. It is exactly the way you always made it, including the dressing."

"How can that be?" Jane's eyes filled with tears before she rested her head in her hands. "I don't remember."

Ellie was out of her chair, crouching by Jane within seconds. "It's okay. You will remember. Lots of times people with amnesia will perform tasks or say things that they don't remember doing. It means your memories are still intact and we just need to find the key to unlock them."

Jane looked at the woman next to her. The sound of her voice was soothing, with conviction behind her words. "Do you really think that will happen?"

"It is my hope that your memories will all return."

"But you don't know that."

"In my heart I do. This coming Friday when we get a brain scan and a complete medical work up, we will know more."

"I'm not looking forward to that," Jane said, her voice shaking.

Ellie stood and took Jane's hand. "If you are to get your memory back, we need to start by looking into your head injury."

Jane pulled her hand away. "What if I refuse?"

"That is your choice," Ellie said, with a shrug. "It is up to you whether you want to remember or not. I will never force you to do anything."

Jane considered the words. Something told her that what Ellie said was the truth. At Salvation she'd had no choice or say in what was being done to her. During the past week that she'd been in the house with Ellie, she'd grown to realize that not everyone was out to control her. Here she was in charge and that made all the difference. "I want to remember and if doing tests will make that happen, then I'm in."

Ellie leaned in and gently hugged Jane's head close and stroked her hair. "I'm glad."

Chapter Twelve

Ellie ran her hand down Jane's arm. During the past couple of days, Jane had allowed the occasional touch without shying away, making Ellie's hope of Syd returning all the more strong. "Are you ready for today?"

Jane blew out a breath. "Yes. I admit I'm nervous but I am ready to find out what's going on with my head so I can get my memory back." A small smile formed on her lips. "Mostly I'm hungry."

"As soon as the test is done, I promise you we will have something to eat. Do you like hamburgers?"

Jane's forehead creased. "I don't know. Can't remember ever having eaten a hamburger, although I've heard of them."

What could Ellie say to that? Syd always loved hamburgers and would drag Ellie all over, proclaiming that they'd eventually find hamburger nirvana. "Well today, after the tests, you will find out."

"You said that they will give me a shot with some sort of dye."

"Yes. It will give the radiologist a clearer picture. Would you like me to discuss with you what will happen again?"

"No. I read about it last night. Not sure I like the idea of going inside a tube. It's kind of frightening."

"Only your head will be in there. There won't be a lot of noise, mostly a whirring sound but nothing to be afraid of."

"Are you sure you can't be in there with me?"

"Yes, but I'll be watching through a window. I'll show you where I will be when we go into the room." Ellie squeezed Jane's hand. "Trust me. I won't let anything happen to you." Jane shrugged and Ellie felt a stab to her heart. "You do trust me, don't you?"

Jane's eyes looked at the floor. "I wish I could tell you what you want to hear, but the last person I trusted let horrible things happen to me."

"I'm not Dr. Rojas, Jane. I'll protect you with my life," Ellie said with conviction.

"Is it time to go?"

"Yes, it is." Ellie closed her eyes and felt the sting of tears. She wouldn't let Jane see her cry or know how deeply hurt she was. Jane had no memory of their love or life together and although she kept reminding herself that it wasn't Jane's fault, the words still upset her.

†

Jane gripped the interior handle of Ellie's car tighter the closer they got to the hospital. Memories of what had happened to her at Salvation haunted her and she felt her chest tighten. Her heart felt like it was going to explode and terror began to consume her. "I can't breathe," she cried.

"Slow down your breathing," Ellie replied. "I'll find a place to park."

"I can't." Jane's wild eyes looked at the street. "I need to get out of here. Now."

"Hold on. I see a parking lot ahead. Please try to relax. Remember the breathing exercise we do for your pain? In through your nose, hold the breath, and then out through your mouth."

"I think I'm going to die," Jane whispered.

"No, you're not. Just hang in there." Ellie pulled into a parking spot and stopped the car.

When a hand reached out to touch her, Jane recoiled and moved as close to the door as possible. "Don't touch me." She began fumbling for the door handle to open the door.

"Jane. Listen to me. You are having a panic attack. You need to concentrate on your breathing." Ellie lowered the back windows, letting fresh air fill the car. "You're safe. No one is going to hurt you," she said in a soft, soothing voice. "Look at me, Jane. I'm your friend. Look at me."

Jane heard the words and tried to slow her breathing. *She kept repeating the words in through your nose, hold the breath, and then out through your mouth* in her head and felt the heaviness in her chest recede.

"There you go. Just keep doing that, Jane. Let your body relax and go with the feeling."

Jane finally let go of her grip on the door handle and looked at Ellie. "I'm sorry. I thought I could do this but I can't…I just can't let that test happen." Her body was still trembling and the feeling of being trapped was skirting the edges of her rational thought.

"That's okay. Whenever you are ready, we can reschedule." Ellie pulled out her phone. "Let me give them a call and cancel then we can go get something to eat.

"Thank you. I'm sorry."

"No need to be sorry. I'm on your side and we will do everything according to your wishes and needs." Ellie reached out and placed her hand on Jane's. "Are you feeling better now?"

Jane pulled her hand away. "Yes."

Stupid, stupid, stupid. I should have never pushed her into the test. Ellie berated herself. *She isn't the person I knew. She isn't Syd anymore.* The thought stabbed at her heart. The Syd she knew was strong and confident ready to face any challenge full on. Jane was the opposite—frightened of her own shadow, seeing everything as a threat. She knew that Syd was in there and it was just a matter of reaching her. The fear that Syd would never return to her weighed heavily on her heart. Perhaps hamburgers at Archie's Hideaway would help nudge her memory.

†

Jane looked at Ellie when the car stopped in front of a rundown building. "What is this place?" she asked.

"According to a good friend, this is where we'll get the best hamburgers around," Ellie replied.

"It doesn't look very clean."

"On the outside but trust me, inside it is like a comfortable home and the food is excellent."

"If you say so."

Ellie smiled and opened her door. "Come on. You must be starving."

"I am." Jane stepped out of the car. The smells that greeted her made her stomach grumble and her mouth water. Her eyes took in the building again and she gulped down the uneasiness she'd been feeling all morning.

†

Inside, the atmosphere was homey with red and white checkered table cloths on square wooden tables and chairs that were surprisingly comfortable. The walls were made of cedar planks, and license plates from around the world adorned them along with some pictures that appeared to be from the turn of the century.

"Do you like it?" Ellie asked. Her memories returned to the first time Syd brought her there. She thought, like Jane, that the place was a dump but once inside everything changed. She loved the atmosphere and the fact that a beautiful, confident, and smart woman brought her there. As the memory filled her with warmth, she looked across the table to Jane. The anxiety of earlier had all but disappeared from her face but her lips were still held in a grim line. "Do you want to go?'

Jane shook her head. "No. It just seems rather dark in here."

Ellie looked around. In all the times she'd been to Archie's, she'd never noticed that it was dimly lit but now she noticed that it was. "Does that bother you?"

"It's a bit creepy to me but I'm ready to try a hamburger." The tone of Jane's voiced belied her confident words.

"What'll it be, ladies?" a petite woman with both arms sleeved in tattoos asked.

"Two Archie burgers with mayo and fries," Ellie said. She had never been a fan of mayonnaise on hamburgers but it was Syd's favorite and she prayed it would be Jane's too. "I just know you're gonna love it."

"It smells good…greasy but good."

The last time Ellie was there, she was with Syd. Now, she sat across from the same woman who called herself Jane. It was so surreal. If she didn't know better, Ellie would think it was a dream. Her ears perked up when she heard a song playing in the background—their song. "Do you like this song?"

Jane frowned. "I don't know what it is. What is this song?"

"The title is *I Run to You* and Lady Antebellum sings it."

"I guess it's okay." Jane shrugged. "At Salvation there was only some kind of background music but there were never any words, just a melody. One of the nurses told me it was to help soothe the patients. I never found it to be all that soothing and once I was in my room full time I never heard it again."

"Did you ever leave the room?"

"No. The first month I did. I even played games with the others. That was before—" Jane scrubbed her head with her fingers. Just then the food arrived.

Ellie rubbed her hands together. "Wait till you taste this." She picked up her burger. "Go ahead, dig in, you'll love it."

Jane lifted the bun. "Does it always come with all this stuff on it?" She wrinkled her nose.

"Do you want something else?" Ellie felt her heart sink. "I should have asked. I'm sorry. Let me order you something else."

"No. It's okay. I didn't really know what to expect that's all." Jane picked up the burger and took a bite.

"Well. What do you think?"

Jane chewed then put the sandwich back on the plate. "I like your cooking better." Jane picked up a French fry and put it in her mouth. "This is greasy but sort of good."

Devastation filled Ellie. What she'd hoped would be a homecoming of sorts was a disaster. Jane remembered nothing and Syd's favorite food was apparently abhorrent to her. "This was a bad idea. Let me pay the bill and then we can go back ho…to the house and I'll fix you something I know you will like."

"No. This is fine. I'm sure it is delicious I just don't have a frame of reference for it."

Ellie scraped her chair back and stood. "I'll settle up and we can leave."

"Wait," Jane said. "I really like it."

"No, you don't. There's no sense in wasting time here." Ellie walked away, angry with herself and with Jane. *What was I thinking?* Her hopes that being there would help spark memories were dashed and the realization that Syd was probably lost to her forever loomed heavy in her heart. It was time to let Syd go, regroup, and make new memories with Jane.

†

The ride back to the house happened in silence. Jane was exhausted from a day that started with hope but soon turned into something she couldn't understand. The thought of getting the brain scan and the hope of starting to regain her memory was something she had anticipated with an expectation of positive results. Yet, something happened to her on the ride to the hospital that terrified her. She suddenly found herself back at Salvation, facing the torment she suffered daily. Where that had come from she didn't know and it had caught her completely off guard.

Jane saw the devastation in Ellie's face when they had lunch and she knew that she was somehow responsible. She didn't know what the importance the lunch place held or why Ellie was so set on her liking the food but she suspected it had to do with Syd. *How I wish I could remember her— us— and see her smile again.*

The ringing of the doorbell made her jump. She looked around and listened for Ellie but she wasn't there. The bell rang again and Jane took tentative steps toward the door, determined not to let fear rule her life any more.

Ellie appeared from out of nowhere. "I'll get it."

Jane watched as Ellie looked through the peep hole.

"What the hell." Ellie pulled the door open.

Not able to see who was there along with a tingle that prickled her neck, Jane took several steps backward and listened.

"What are you doing here?" Ellie's angry voice said.

"I wanted to see you and explain," a voice answered.

Jane knew the voice and ran to the door. "Dr. Rojas." She engulfed the woman in a fierce hug and held onto her as if her life depended on it. "I knew you'd come."

Ellie swallowed hard. After all the torture Maya Rojas had put Jane through, it appeared that Jane forgave it all. It was clear that there was something between the two women that she had failed to see.

But how could I have known? I never saw them together or thought to ask Jane about Maya. I should have.

"Why aren't you in jail?" Her words were filled with venom.

Jane let go of Maya and stepped back. "You were in jail?"

Maya nodded. "I came here to explain."

"Explain what?" Ellie sneered at the woman. "How you kept Jane a prisoner so Dr. Addison could do experiments on her?" She turned to Jane. "Did you know she did that to you?"

"No, she tried to stop him," Jane cried.

Ellie moved so she was in front of Maya and facing Jane. "No. She allowed it to happen. She kept you there at Salvation, never alerting the authorities that they had someone who had amnesia and that they couldn't identify. Instead, she made up some fictitious husband. Did he visit you, Jane? Did he bring the kids you supposedly shared?" Ellie felt her blood boiling and the result was a terrified looking Jane.

"I'm sorry if I've upset you," she whispered. "But Dr. Rojas was no friend to you."

Jane's eyes darted to Maya. "Is that true?" she asked in a tremulous voice.

Ellie swung around staring at Maya, daring her to lie.

"If you'll let me in, I'll explain."

Jane placed her hand on Ellie's back. "I'd like to hear what she has to say."

Ellie didn't know what to do. She wanted to protect Jane from the woman standing in front of her yet she knew that Jane deserved to know the whole truth. "You can come in but know that I know everything and with the first lie that comes out of your mouth, I will drag you out of here." Her eyes fixed squarely on Maya. "Is that clear?"

"Yes. I promise nothing but the truth. Both of you deserve that."

†

When Maya sat on the couch and Jane chose to sit next to her, Ellie's hackles rose. From what she'd seen at the door, Jane was probably enamored with the woman.

Stockholm syndrome. She was, after all, the one who treated her and bonded with her for seven months. I, on the other hand, am nothing but a stranger. I found that out first hand at lunch.

Understanding didn't help—jealousy flared. She tamped it down, knowing that now was not the time for destructive emotions. If she was going to get Jane out from under Maya's spell, she'd have to use all her wiles to make that happen.

"Could I have a glass of water please," Maya asked.

Ellie glared at the woman. "This isn't a social visit."

"I'll get it." Jane jumped up and hurried off toward the kitchen.

"It's obvious that she has some sort of attachment to you so don't you dare try to take advantage of that. Take this as my warning. Do not hurt her any more than you already have."

"I certainly read you all wrong, Elinor."

Ellie moved her head slightly and took out her phone. "To be on the safe side, I'll call Captain Barth and see if he can join us."

"No. Don't. He already knows what I am going to tell you."

"Then it shouldn't be a problem if I call him, should it." Ellie pressed the button and put her phone on speaker. "Hello, Captain Barth, this is Elinor Scott."

"Dr. Scott, what can I do for you?"

"Maya Rojas has just showed up at my door. I thought you might want to join us or I can just leave the phone on speaker and you can hear what she has to say."

"Dr. Rojas, do you remember the agreement you made with the police?"

"Yes, I do."

"Well, I don't," Ellie interjected.

"I cannot comment on that, Ellie, but I'll listen to make sure she follows the agreement to the letter."

147

Jane came back in the room with a glass of water and sat so close to Maya that their thighs were touching. "What's going on?"

Ellie laid her phone on the table next to her chair. "Jane is here and Dr. Rojas was just getting ready to tell us her story." She smiled at Jane before glaring at the woman next to her. "Go ahead, Rojas, you're up."

Maya took a drink of the water, cleared her throat, and smiled at Jane. "Thank you for this." She held up the glass.

"I'm waiting," Ellie said.

"For years a man named Alexander Bennington was my mentor and confidant. He made sure I had the best internship, the best practice, and the best profile in my field. As the years went by, he was always there for me...when my parents passed, when my younger brother was killed by a gang, and for every other life event, he was there."

"Touching," Ellie scoffed.

Maya nodded. "It was. He was everything to me so when he told me there was a position opening that would be perfect for me and my career, I jumped at the chance." She let out a long sigh. "I became the director of the up and coming facility for rehab known as Salvation. He told me that oftentimes celebrities would be admitted and that they needed anonymity so they would be admitted under one doctor's name and there would be a special wing just for them.

"It was a year before anyone like that was admitted. I was ready to do an admittance exam but was told it was already taken care of. I argued that we needed to follow protocol but then Alexander called me and told me to admit the person with no questions asked."

Maya lowered her head. "I knew it was wrong, but I let it happen." She shrugged. "After that I learned that what happened in the other wing was none of my concern. They told me it was a separate entity and Salvation was used as a portal to get there. As time went by, whenever they said that someone was for the specialty wing, I just admitted them."

"How did Jane fit into this? She wasn't in that *specialty* wing." Ellie doubted every word coming from Maya's mouth but since the captain wasn't voicing any objections, she figured it was the truth. *Unless she lied her pants off to get out of jail.*

"One day Dr. Addison came in with a patient—Jane. I'd never seen him before and knew he wasn't on staff and asked why he was there. He handed me a letter from Alexander that directed me to admit Jane, who he said had a severe head injury complicated by amnesia. The letter also said that Addison was granted privileges at Salvation and he was to be admitted into the facility at all times."

"And you just let that happen? You're a doctor, for God's sake. How could you?" Ellie was incensed by the story so far. "Syd's story made the national news. Why didn't anyone notify us? Surely someone at Salvation heard that news. Or is the entire staff in cahoots with what you were doing?"

"At first she wore a mask and a cap when she interacted with the staff and other patients. I told them that she had breathing problems and needed the filter the mask provided. After that I kept her isolated and only the staff that were paid to keep their mouths shut saw her."

"Therein the non-disclosure clause."

"I remember the dark glasses and not being able to breathe with that mask on," Jane said in a flat tone. "After that, they kept me in the room and they never turned on the lights. The only time that happened was when...." Jane looked at Maya. "When I was in the room alone with her."

"You did that to her?" Ellie balled her fingers into fists. "What kind of doctor are you?"

Maya raised her head and looked directly at Jane and then at Ellie. "You don't understand. I had no choice. Since I had already compromised my position, I was in danger of losing not only my job but my license. I did what they told me."

She bent her head again. "Jane had been there a month before Addison returned. It was one night when Jane was having terrible pain in her head. He just appeared, insisting that I give her a shot to sedate her. I refused and he told me I had no choice. That either I could administer the shot or he would find someone who would.

"I reluctantly gave her the shot but not the full dose. He waited but she never went completely under and he stormed out after telling me the next time I'd better make sure she was out or I'd be sorry. Again he showed up one night when she was in desperate need of relief. I gave her the full dose that time because she was in so much pain and I couldn't stand to see her suffer. It didn't take long and she was out. It was then that he attached that horrible machine to her head. I protested and he turned on me and shoved me out of the room."

Jane patted Maya's leg. "I knew you were trying to help me when he came. I don't blame you."

Ellie stood. "You don't blame her? Are you kidding me? She's the reason you don't remember who you are. Had she come forward and told the authorities that you were there, we could have helped you and not put you through the torture she allowed." Ellie pointed angrily at Maya. "She's the reason, Jane, for everything."

"She protected me. She was the only one who cared about me," Jane cried. "The only one. You certainly weren't there, so how would you know."

"I would have been had I known." Ellie's voice softened. "Jane, listen to me. Dr. Rojas didn't protect you. What she did was to let them hold you prisoner in that place."

"No. She told me I had no family."

Ellie snorted. "Your records showed you had a husband and three kids. She lied to you."

She went to Jane and knelt in front of her. "You do have family and they would have been there for you had they known." Ellie touched her chest. "I would have been at your side. Instead I walked around in a coma of sorrow, wondering where you were. We didn't know if you were dead or alive, and it is all thanks to this kind and caring woman." Ellie swiped at her eyes. "Dr. Rojas is not your friend or savior. She didn't report a person with amnesia to the authorities. If she had, your parents and I would have been there immediately. Instead you languished for seven months while this so called doctor who you think was so kind to you let Addison perform his experiments on you."

"No, that can't be true." Jane looked at Maya.

"It's all true, Jane." Maya shook her head. "You were making improvements in remembering and I was hopeful you'd make a full recovery until Addison started his *treatment*s on you." Maya clutched Jane's hand. "I am so sorry."

"Get your hands off her," Ellie demanded as she stood. "Get out of our house and never come back." Ellie picked up her phone. "I don't know what kind of deal you made with her, Captain, but she should be in a jail cell for the rest of her life for what she's done to Syd."

"I agree, but it is out of my hands. The authorities from Overton called in the state investigators and it is now in the hands of the state Crime Investigation Department. I can tell you that Maya Rojas has had her license to practice medicine rescinded and she is cooperating in the investigation."

Ellie took the phone off speaker. "That is not good enough. I'll speak with you later. Thank you for your time, Captain." She ended the call before turning and glaring at Maya. "Please leave. You're not welcome here."

Maya gave Jane a gentle hug. "I'm sorry. Please forgive me."

Jane, looking like she was in a daze, said nothing.

Ellie opened the front door and nodded in its direction. "Don't ever make any contact with her again. I hope that the damage you've done to her haunts you till your dying day. Not only have you destroyed who she was but you've ruined the lives of all of us who love her. I hope you rot in hell. Now, get out!"

Maya nodded and went to the door. "I had no choice."

"You always have choices. There is only one right choice and you failed to choose it."

As soon as Maya was out the door Ellie shut it and locked it.

Jane was still standing by the couch looking dazed and confused.

Ellie made her way quickly to Jane and took her into her arms. It was then that Jane began to sob uncontrollably.

"How could she do that to me?" she sobbed.

"It is simple really. She did it because she could. No one was there to monitor what she was doing so she made her own rules."

"There was one person there that did help me," Jane said.

Ellie motioned to the couch and they sat. "Who was that?"

"A nurse. Her name was Marie. She always seemed to know when the pain would start and she'd come sit with me and talk about her family and her job. She said that by telling me about her life I might remember mine." Jane chewed on her lip. "I didn't remember but it helped ease the pain so I wouldn't need a shot." Jane shivered. "I knew the shot would mean the man with the white hair would come and make the pain worse." She sighed. "I fought it every time but it became too much to take."

Ellie wrapped her arm around Jane's shoulders. "I won't let that happen to you ever again. I met that nurse the first day I was at Salvation and I think she was trying to tell me about you but Dr. Rojas cut her off."

Jane rested her head on Ellie's shoulder. "I'm so tired."

"Close your eyes and I'll be right here when you wake up."

With a yawn, Jane closed her eyes and when her breathing evened out Ellie knew she was asleep

Chapter Thirteen

Three days after Maya visited, the doorbell rang again and Ellie watched as Jane froze before scurrying off to her room. She shook her head and walked to the door, knowing full well who was there.

"Good morning, you two."

Anita hugged Ellie. "Any change?"

"No. She's been hiding out in her room ever since she arrived. The only time she comes out is to eat or go out back and sit on the patio."

"She knew we were coming right?" Craig asked.

Ellie nodded. "She might look like Syd but that is where the similarities end. The once confident woman we knew is now afraid of her own shadow."

"They should hog-tie that woman to a fence and let wild animals feed on her," Craig said bitterly. "How they ever let such an evil person out of jail is beyond me."

"Unfortunately, deals are made all the time," Ellie said.

Craig took Ellie's hand. "You should know that Addison made bail the next day and has disappeared. I didn't tell you then because you had so much to deal with that I didn't want to add anything else. Especially that."

Ellie's hand went to her mouth. "My God. When will it ever end?"

"I wish I knew." Craig pulled Ellie into a hug.

Human contact was what she craved and Ellie melted into the embrace.

"Is she in her room?" Anita asked.

"Yes."

"Let me go see if I can coax her into joining us."

Ellie smiled. "Good luck. I hope you can."

†

Anita knocked gently on the door and opened it. In the darkened room, she spied the form of her daughter huddled under the covers. "Good morning, darling. How are you feeling this morning?"

She moved toward the window and pulled open the curtain. "Let's let some light in."

"No. Close it," Jane mumbled.

"Nonsense. You can't spend your life in this room. It's time to pull yourself together and join us. Ellie has put together a lovely brunch for us to share." Anita walked to the bed and pulled the covers back. "Time to get up," she said."

"They'll come again. It's not safe," Jane cried.

"That's crazy talk. Haven't you noticed that Ellie would give up her life to keep you safe." Anita paused. "And so would we."

"She would? You would?"

"Okay, that's enough," Anita said in her sternest but most loving voice.

Jane's eyes widened.

"I get it. Something happened to you and you lost your memory but the core person you are is still there. I don't believe that when you look at Ellie or us you can't see the love we have for you."

"That's the problem."

Anita frowned. "Enlighten me."

"I have no frame of reference for what love is."

"How does Ellie make you feel?"

Jane smiled. "When I'm around her I feel safe...protected. She is so kind to me and is always there to help me when I get afraid or confused."

"Is that how Dr. Rojas made you feel."

"No!"

Confused, Anita looked at her daughter. From what Ellie had told her about the meeting with the doctor it sounded as if Jane was infatuated with Maya. "I thought you liked her," she said cautiously.

"Except for one nurse, she was the only one who took any time with me. I really thought she was trying to help me until she let that man give me more pain." Jane swiped at an errant tear. "I had no one else."

Wrapping her arms around her daughter, Anita rubbed her back. "You're safe now. We won't let anything happen to you. We all love you."

"I wish I could feel the same."

Anita pulled back and put a hand over Jane's heart. "It's here, all you need to do is let it out."

"It can't be that simple," Jane said, shaking her head.

"But it is, my darling. It is. When I see you looking at Ellie, your eyes follow her and most of the time there is a tiny smile on your face. I think to myself that the love you had for her is still there just waiting to burst forth."

"The warm feelings I have for her are love?"

"Yes. The beginnings."

Jane cocked her head to one side. "Huh. I didn't know."

"What do you say we get you washed up and in some clean clothes and you join your dad and Ellie. Whatever she cooked sure smelled scrumptious."

"She always has been a good cook," Jane said absently as she crawled off the bed.

"Yes, she has." A wide smile filled Anita's face.

†

To Ellie, Jane was the most relaxed she'd been since they returned home from Salvation. She was animated, funny at times, and it seemed as though she was settling in, finally. It was obvious that whatever Anita had said to her daughter caused the change.

A curious look filled Jane's face. "Where are Jill, Terry and the kids?"

All the eyes at the table turned to Jane.

"Why do you ask?" Ellie looked at Anita in question.

Anita shook her head.

"Don't they usually come to Sunday brunch?" Jane's eyes moved from one person to the next. "What?'

"How do you know that?" Anita asked.

Jane's face went blank for a minute before she shrugged. "I just figured they would be here too."

Ellie's mind worked furiously trying to remember if she had mentioned that her sister's family usually joined them on Sunday. She was certain she hadn't. Then she wondered if Anita or Jill had said anything to her while at Salvation. "They usually do join us but they couldn't today," Ellie answered.

"How many kids does Jill have?" Anita asked.

Jane cocked her head to the side. "A boy and a girl." Her eyes searched her mother's. "Right?"

157

A broad smile filled Anita's face. "Yes, my darling, that is right."

Craig pushed back his chair and stood. "I'll clear the table."

"And I'll help," Jane said, as she stood.

Once the two left the room, Ellie turned to Anita. "Did you tell her that they joined us on Sundays?"

"No. I thought you had but I could tell by the look on your face you hadn't." Anita's face brightened. "Did you tell her Jill had kids?"

Ellie shook her head. "Maybe Jill did when she was sitting with her in that horrible place." She pulled her phone out of her pocket. "Good morning, sis. Brunch was good. We missed you guys. Yeah, I know it would have been too much for her. Next Sunday for sure. Question. Did you tell Jane that you all usually came for Sunday brunch? I didn't think so. She wondered where you were. Did you tell her that you had children? Huh, that's curious. She told us you had a boy and a girl." Ellie smiled. "Yes, Syd's in there and wants to come out. Okay, talk with you later. Bye."

"She never told her, did she?" Anita's voice was laced with excitement.

"No," Ellie said cautiously. "Unfortunately, I don't think it will all come flooding back to her in one fell swoop. There is every possibility that by tomorrow she will forget. We need to run tests but until she is willing to do that, there is no way of knowing what the damage to her brain is."

Anita smiled. "Listen to them out there." Laughter was coming from the kitchen. "Being in the kitchen with her after brunch was always Craig's favorite time. He always looked forward to his one on one time with her." She swiped an errant tear from her cheek. "She's coming back to us. I can feel it in my bones."

"From your lips to God's ears." Ellie looked at the doorway as Jane and Craig returned. "It's your day, Jane, what would you like to do next?"

Jane scratched her nose. "Hmm, after all that food, how about we go to the zoo and walk it off," she said in a shy, uncertain voice.

"Excellent," Craig said, beaming. "We haven't been there in a while."

Jane grinned. "The monkeys have probably missed us."

Everyone laughed.

"Remember how we'd stand in front of that one monkey who would always come right up to the bars and make kissing sounds?" Anita asked. "Come on, let's go." She turned to Ellie. "Maybe Jill and her family can join us."

"Yes. Please call her," Jane said.

Ellie's heart filled with hope.

Jane woke up feeling more refreshed than she could ever remember—of course that was only eight months ago. She thought of Ellie and let out a sigh of contentment. The woman often made her smile and the warm feelings that accompanied that smile were beginning to become familiar. The debilitating pain she had at Salvation no longer made her want to cut her head off.

Thanks to Ellie.

Jane knew it was time to move forward but the thought of anyone—even Ellie—probing her brain terrified her. The easy way was to keep refusing. She knew she could tell Ellie she was afraid or have another panic attack like last time and Ellie would not make her do it. But did she want to keep living her life in limbo? The resounding answer was no.

She sprang out of bed and headed for the bathroom with a new resolve. The warm water cascading down her body made Jane close her eyes as she relished the feeling. In the month that she'd been living with Ellie, Jane found that she had a heightened state of awareness. The staff at Salvation never offered her a leisurely shower. It was always get in, get out while someone stood by watching her. Now that Jane understood it wasn't the norm, the realization that she was indeed a prisoner at Salvation often took her breath away. During her time there she didn't know differently but being with Ellie showed her what freedom was and she liked it.

Stepping out of the shower, she wiped a towel across the steamed up mirror and looked at herself. The face she saw looking back at her was rested and the gaunt look she'd first seen when she'd arrived at the home she was sharing with Ellie were gone. Her body was no longer scarecrow-like but shapely. The workouts she'd done with Ellie had helped build her muscles and she now looked like the person in the pictures. Cognizant of the changes during the past month, not only to her body but her mind, she knew what needed to be done.

†

Ellie looked up and smiled. "Are you ready for some breakfast?"

"Yes. For some reason, I am famished this morning."

"You look refreshed. A good night's sleep, I take it." Ellie noticed a glow to Jane that she hadn't seen before.

"The best yet." Jane sniffed the air. "Do I smell French toast?'

"You do. Take a seat and I'll bring it in."

Jane touched Ellie's wrist. "No. Let me serve you this morning for a change." She tilted her head. "You're always doing for me. Let me do something for you. Okay?"

"Okay." Ellie sat at the table and watched as Jane walked into the kitchen.

Was she humming? Yes, that is definitely humming. Wonder what made that happen.

Jane returned with a plate of French toast along with crispy bacon. She leaned over Ellie's shoulder and placed two of each on her plate.

Ellie watched in fascination as Jane pulled the plate from the end of the table where she usually sat and placed it in front of the chair next to hers.

"Do you mind if I sit here instead?"

"No. No, not at all." Ellie swallowed hard. When Jane leaned to put the food on her plate, she'd had to close her eyes at the closeness. She had to catch her breath when Jane's breast made contact with her back. *Now this. Wow.* "You're in a good mood this morning."

"I feel good. When I woke up this morning I had a strange feeling."

"Like what?"

"It was as if everything had righted itself."

"In what way?" Ellie's stomach roiled as she braced herself for what was to come.

"I'm not sure. It's like a fog has cleared and I can look back at my time at Salvation and see it for what it was—a prison." Jane shrugged. "If that makes any sense at all."

Ellie cleared her throat that was suddenly dry. "It makes perfect sense. You needed time to process everything that happened there, sorting out the good and the bad. What was real and what was imagined."

"Exactly." Jane put her fork down and gave Ellie a contemplative look. "If I ever want a chance at getting back to who I was, I need to make a change."

"What kind of change?" Again her stomach was queasy. Is she trying to say she's leaving? God, I don't think I could take that. Not now that I just found her.

"To no longer be afraid." Jane sucked in a breath. "I want to do the test...the brain scan thing."

Ellie's eyes widened. "Are you sure?"

"Yes. Will you arrange it for me?"

"Of course I will. Any particular time frame?"

"As soon as possible." Jane grinned. "But not before I finish this delicious breakfast. You really are a great cook. There is just the right amount of vanilla in the toast and the bacon is the way I like it. Thank you."

"You're welcome." Ellie reached out and took Jane's hand. "I'm glad you've decided to do this. It will help in finding out what is going on in that pretty head of yours."

Jane looked away. "You think I'm pretty."

"Yes. Yes, I do. I've always thought that." The blush was evident on Jane's face and Ellie squeezed her hand. "It's hard for me sometimes to be around you and not just stare. That's how beautiful you are to me."

"I wish I could be *her* for you," Jane whispered.

"I like who you are, Jane. Let's see what the test shows and we can go from there." Ellie took Jane's chin and turned it so they were looking into one another's eyes. "You remember more than you think."

Jane frowned. "I do?"

"Yes. There are times when you do things without thinking about them just as you did in the past. For example, no one told you that Jill had two kids much less that one was a boy and the other a girl but you knew somehow."

"Maybe I saw a picture of them."

"Where? The only picture I have of her family is in my wallet."

"Hmm." Jane's forehead creased as if she were deep in thought. "So you're saying that Syd is still in here." She pointed to her head.

Ellie smiled. "Yes, in there and in your heart."

"I guess we will see."

"Yes, we will. Once we've finished breakfast, I'll make the arrangements."

Chapter Fourteen

The closer they got to the hospital the more Jane trembled inside. Ellie had held her hand during the entire journey except when she needed both hands to drive. That gave Jane some comfort but did not dispel her anxiety. By the time Ellie parked the car, Jane's free hand was locked into a permanent ball.

"Are you ready?" Ellie asked, patting Jane's thigh.

Jane mustered all the bravado she could and nodded. "Yes," she whispered. The next thing she knew, Ellie had opened the door and was crouching down next to her.

"Sweetheart, it is going to be okay. I'll be with you all the way, just like we talked about. While the test is being done you will be able to hear and talk to me. You won't be alone and I won't let anyone hurt you."

Jane looked at Ellie, still trying to process why she didn't hear the door open. "I didn't hear the door open, I must really be out of it," she murmured.

"You're doing just fine. Come on," Ellie stood and held out her hand. "Go with me and let's get started on your road to recovery."

Jane took the hand—it was warm and strong—and exited the car. "You will be there with me?"

"I promise I'll be right by your side except during the CAT scan."

Drawing in a deep breath, Jane agreed. "Okay, then. Let's go."

†

Ellie held Jane's hand all the way across the parking lot and into the hospital. Many of the staff greeted Ellie warmly, telling her they were glad to see her back. Jane surmised that Ellie had been a valued member of the staff before she moved on to Salvation.

Good thing she did or I'd probably be a vegetable by now, she thought.

Hand in hand they continued on through the building until they finally found their way to the CAT scan area. Ellie pushed open the door to reveal an empty waiting room.

"Good morning, Dr. Scott. They're all ready for you. Just let me call back there and let them know you're here," a woman with black hair and glasses sitting behind a counter said. "It's good to see you back."

"Thank you, Evelyn."

A second later a door opened and a tall woman with strawberry blond hair wearing a lab coat over black slacks and a white shirt smiled at them. "Jane, are you ready?" the radiologist asked. "My name is Gretchen Benoit and I am the radiologist who will be reading and interpreting your scan today. Along with Ellie here."

Jane clutched Ellie's hand, feeling her body begin to tremble.

"Don't be afraid. I'll be with you all the way. Remember what we talked about and what's going to happen?" Ellie asked.

Jane nodded.

165

Ellie smiled and squeezed Jane's hand. "Let's find out what's going on in that pretty head of yours." She looked at Gretchen. "Thanks for doing this for me and letting us come in before the masses."

"Not a problem. I'm happy to help out." She pointed to a chair. "Please sit there so I can get an IV line going. Then I'll inject you with the contrast material once we get in the room."

Jane swallowed hard but sat in the chair.

"Nothing to be nervous about, Jane, I've done this a million times. Just relax and all you will feel is a little prick then I'll be done," Gretchen said in a soothing voice.

Jane was still holding Ellie's hand as the IV was inserted. "I didn't feel much," she said and smiled at the radiologist.

"Ellie do you want to take her into the room and get her in place while I set things up?"

"Sure. Come on, Jane. This is going to be quick and easy." Still holding Jane's hand Ellie walked with her into a room with the long narrow machine that was hollow in the middle.

Jane's eyes widened and she looked at Ellie. "I don't know if I can do this," she whispered.

"If you want we can leave, sweetheart. Just say the word."

Jane saw the disappointment in Ellie's eyes but she knew that if she wanted to leave no one would stop her.

"No. I'm good."

She bent down and gazed at the doughnut-shaped opening. "That looks just like the picture you showed me."

Ellie grinned. "Remember what I said about them fitting your head into a brace so you can't move your head."

"Yeah, I remember." Jane sucked in a deep breath. "Not sure I'm comfortable with that but I'm willing to give it a try."

"That's my girl."

"I need you to lie down here." Ellie pointed to a long extension that resembled a gutter.

After getting in position and having her arms resting on extensions, Ellie secured her head in the brace.

Gretchen entered the room "I'm going to inject you with a contrasting agent now. You're going to feel a warm sensation but that should be all," she said as she injected the dye.

Jane's eyes tracked to Ellie who nodded. "It will be fine."

"Just remember that it's important that you stay completely still while the scan is running. Make sure to hold your breath when asked. Any kind of movement can skew the image." Gretchen patted Jane's shoulder. "You ready to start?"

Jane reached for Ellie. "You'll be close by, right?"

Ellie pointed to a large window in front of the machine. "I'll be right in there and will be in voice communication with you. There's nothing to be afraid of."

"Okay," Jane said in a tremulous voice.

"Just keep your eyes focused on me and it will be finished before you know it. If you need me just call out to me and I'll hear you."

"Will do."

Jane never took her eyes off Ellie, who was standing behind the glass right where she said she would. The machine asked her to hold her breath and she did and she heard the whirring sounds the machine made and just like that the table was sliding out and Ellie was coming back in the room.

†

From the other room Ellie watched Jane intently as the machine started. "How are you doing?" she asked Jane.

"A little nervous but I'm good. I can do this."

Ellie smiled. *She sounded so much like Syd.* "You're doing great. Try and remember the video you watched about what is happening.

Ellie watched as the picture of Jane's brain began to build. She saw nothing out of the ordinary that would cause the loss of memory.

The door opened and both Gretchen and Ellie turned to see Perry Stanley whose specialty was neurosurgery coming in the room. "I had a few minutes so I thought I'd see if you find anything."

"We just started, Perry," Gretchen said. "So far I haven't seen anything out of the ordinary."

Ellie's eyes narrowed. "Wait. What the hell is that?"

Perry came and stood next to the two woman and running a hand across his chin. "Whatever it is, it doesn't belong there."

"Ellie." Jane's voice resonated in the room.

"I'm here. How are you doing?"

"My head hurts a little."

Ellie looked at Perry and cut off the voice to Jane. "Can whatever that is make that happen?"

Perry shook his head. "I don't think so but until we find out what that is, we can't rule out what it will do."

Ellie flipped the voice back on. "How bad is the pain? Remember we did the scale of one to ten for your pain level…what number is it?"

"Right now it is a one."

"Can you hang in there for me a little while longer, sweetheart."

"I'll try."

"Good. Let me know if it gets to a three, okay."

"Yes."

A prickling on her neck made Ellie nervous. "I don't have a good feeling about this, Perry. Is there enough there for you?"

"To do an in depth study, no. This scan shouldn't have any adverse effects. I think it will be safe to complete the test." He looked at the monitor. "Won't be much longer."

Ellie couldn't stand the idea of the scan hurting Jane but she knew Perry was right. Had it been an MRI, Jane's brain would have been scrambled almost immediately if the object was metal. "How long after will you know what it is?"

Perry smiled. "You know that answer as well as I do. We won't know anything until we take it out."

Ellie shook her head. "Given her recent history I'm not sure I can sell her on that."

"Okay, it's finished," Gretchen said.

†

"All done," Ellie said as she walked into the room. "You did awesome. I'm so proud of you. You just need to lay there a bit longer while Gretchen takes a look at the images."

"It all looks good. We're done. She can get up now." Gretchen's voice filled the room.

"Okay, let's get you out of the harness." Ellie pulled at the Velcro and released the head gear. "Get up slowly and sit there for a bit before you stand."

Jane did as she was told and moments later she took Ellie's hand and stood. "Now what?"

"How about we go get something to eat."

"I'd like that."

"That wasn't all that bad," Jane said as they got in Ellie's car. "I didn't like my head being strapped down. It kept feeling like the strap was going to slide up my head."

"I've heard that before," Ellie said, pushing the button to start the car. She reached and patted Jane's arm. "I'm really proud of you, sweetheart."

Jane smiled as the now familiar warm feeling spread through her body. She liked it when Ellie called her sweetheart. She'd been saying that a lot lately. Her thoughts turned to the CAT scan and the question that she was afraid to ask.

Suck it up and just ask her. "Did you find anything?"

Ellie put the car back into park and turned slightly. "Yes. They implanted some sort of device in your brain."

"That is what makes my headaches?"

"I think so. Or at least it contributes to them." Ellie took Jane's hand. "The only way to know is to take it out."

Jane gasped. "I can't let you do that."

"I know. Let's give it some time then we can discuss it again. I think that machine Addison used has something to do with it. Your headaches aren't anywhere as severe as when you were at Salvation, are they?"

"Not even close."

"Then we need to find out what, if anything, the state bureau of investigation discovered about the device." Ellie put the car in gear. "Where do you want to go eat?"

Jane covered her rumbling stomach. "I'd like to give that hamburger place another try." Her eyes searched Ellie's. "Is that okay?"

"More than okay."

Chapter Fifteen

Ellie impatiently tapped her pen against the desk. She'd been on the phone all day trying to get information on the instrument that Spencer Addison used on Jane's head. Now that it was confirmed that Jane had something implanted within her brain, it was essential to find out what the function of the rectangular box was.

Jane was reluctant to have brain surgery and Ellie couldn't blame her since there was no way of knowing how the object would react if disturbed. She'd not allow any sort of operation until they had all the facts.

"Hello, this is Janet Easterday."

"Yes, Dr. Easterday, this is Elinor Scott. I am the one who obtained the rectangular box associated with the Dr. Sydney Tanner kidnapping."

"Ah, yes. It is good to finally speak with you, Dr. Scott. I've gone through all the reports and the little forensic evidence that was available. The biggest prize was the instrument."

"A recent CAT scan of my patient's brain showed some sort of object implanted in her brain. Can you tell me anything about the device and how it works?"

"What I found, doctor—this is an educated guess on what I've discovered so far—is that it is some sort of electromagnetic device that transmits short pulsing bursts of magnetism followed by a period of de-energizing."

Ellie saw her frown. "I don't understand. For what purpose would something like that be used? I was thinking it was some sort of shock therapy."

"In a way it is."

"What do you mean *in a way*?"

"I can't be a hundred percent sure until I see what you retrieve from her brain, but my theory is that the machine was doing some sort of conditional therapy.

Ellie shook her head. "How can that be? She presented with severe pain in her head, was given Demerol, and only when she was out did they use the machine. Wouldn't she have to be lucid for something like that to work?"

"That would seem logical. Once you send me the object from her brain, I can get a better picture of what the machine was doing."

Ellie let out a long sigh. "Well, that might be a while. Jane is not anxious to have someone operate on her brain."

"That is understandable but until we have that missing piece, I cannot analyze the machine further."

"I understand. I think she will come around at some point." Ellie tapped her pen on her desk. "Will you please fax me your findings so far, along with a direct number that I can reach you at?"

"Of course. Let me check. Yes, I have your information and will be faxing it to you shortly. Please feel free to call me if you have any further ideas or questions."

"Thank you." Ellie ended the call and wondered how she'd convince Jane to let them operate. She smiled. With each passing day, Jane's timid demeanor was slowly morphing into confidence. Traits that were Syd's were slowly making their way to the forefront yet she was still

Jane—shy and vulnerable. With that thought, she pushed back from the desk and went in search of Jane, knowing where she'd find her.

†

Jane was sitting on the patio watching as hummingbirds whizzed their way through the air to feed on the nectar from the red flowers of the trumpet vines. The patio surrounded by the immaculately kept yard and gardens was her favorite place to be. It made her feel grounded and at peace. The sound of the atrium door opening behind her made Jane turn around. She smiled.

"Thought I'd find you out here," Ellie said, as she sat next to Jane. "It's a glorious day, isn't it?"

A hummingbird buzzed by her head and Jane laughed. "They make such a big sound for something so small." She turned at looked at Ellie. "Did Syd like watching birds?"

Ellie raised her eyebrows in what looked like surprise. "Yes, she did. She's the one that planted those vines." She pointed to the flower bed. "And the hummingbird bushes. Hummers were her favorite birds. Once she told me that they always reminded her that you didn't need to be big to be mighty."

"No, you don't." Jane smiled. "Thank you for letting me use the binoculars and the bird book. I find spending time out here very relaxing."

"No need to thank me, Jane. They are yours to keep."

"They belonged to her, didn't they?"

Ellie nodded, then looked away.

Jane reached out and took Ellie's hand. "I'm sorry if I've upset you. This can't be easy for you." She lifted one shoulder. "Seeing me as Syd."

173

"I see you as Jane," Ellie whispered, holding on to the offered hand. "Yes, you look like Syd, but the woman I've come to know and care about is Jane."

"But you'd rather I'd be Syd."

Ellie smiled and squeezed Jane's hand. "I want you to be who you are and to be happy. Are you happy?"

The warmth of Ellie's hand along with the kindness radiating from her face brought peace and contentment into Jane's heart. "Yes, I am happier than I can ever remember." She looked away. "You make me happy."

"I'm glad to hear that for you make me happy too, Jane."

They sat in companionable silence holding hands for a long while. Jane cleared her throat and asked, "Did you ever get to speak with someone from the state Criminal Investigation Department?"

"Finally after jumping through hoops and being on hold forever, I did get to speak with the right person."

"What did you find out?"

"Dr. Easterday is the woman I spoke to and, from what I gather, is the head of the forensic department. She personally undertook the investigation of the machine that Addison used." Ellie rubbed at her eyes. "All she has are theories. She knows how it works but that is all."

Jane heard the disappointment in Ellie's voice. "Is there anything I can do? I could try to remember more about what it was like."

Ellie shook her head. "I don't want you going back to that time. It is too traumatic for you and you've been through too much already. Besides, it would serve no purpose."

"What aren't you telling me?"

"Why would you think that?"

"Because every time you have something to tell me you rub your eyes."

Ellie smiled. "I'm that transparent?"

"Yes."

"The machine works like an electromagnet that sends out pulses then releases them. Dr. Easterday thought that it might be some sort of device that was conditioning your brain to act in the way Addison wanted it to."

"Okay. Is there more?"

"Yes. Once I told her that we found something implanted in your brain and we discussed various scenarios, she said that there was a high likelihood that the machine worked with whatever is in your head."

Jane was quiet for a moment. "Does she want to try using the machine on me?"

"No! I would never let that happen to you." Ellie stood and held out her hand.

Instinctively Jane took the hand and allowed Ellie to pull her up and engulf her in her arms. She closed her eyes as a warm feeling she did not understand filled her before wrapping her arms around Ellie's slender body.

"Tell me," she whispered. Soft lips caressed her hair and Jane leaned into them. "Tell me what I need to do. Please." Ellie held her tighter.

"Take it out."

The soft emotional voice was Jane's undoing. *She's done so much for me how can I refuse her.* "Okay."

Ellie pulled back. "Are you sure? We don't know what it is or what will happen to you if we take it out. The risk is too great."

"If by doing this, we can find out what they were trying to do to me, maybe it will lead to why this all happened in the first place."

"I can't lose you again. Not now." Ellie placed her hands on Jane's cheeks and leaned in.

175

The kiss was unexpected but Jane found herself enjoying the feeling — a strange sensation yet a very familiar one. From a place deep inside, she remembered the soft lips on hers. When Ellie pulled away she knew she wanted more.

"I'm sorry. I shouldn't have done that." Ellie stepped away.

Jane stepped closer and pulled Ellie to her before kissing her again. Pulling away but still holding Ellie, she spoke. "I'm not sorry."

Ellie leaned her forehead against Jane's. "Would you like to go out on a date with me?"

"Yes, I'd love to."

†

Ellie decided that if she and Jane were going to have new memories, they needed to go to places she and Syd never went. Yet Syd's food preferences still colored her choices. When she settled on the small French bistro, Le Petit Dîner, she recalled Syd's aversion to rich food and almost changed her mind. Almost. Jane didn't really care for the burgers even the second time so there was a pretty good chance rich French food would be welcomed. While making the reservations, she touched her lips, remembering the feel of Jane's lips upon hers. She tried to recall the feelings she had kissing Syd and if kissing Jane was the same but she could not. Both certainly were pleasurable.

"Hi, whatcha doin'," Jane said from the doorway.

"I just made dinner reservations. I hope you like French food."

Jane grinned before moving further into the room. "The only reference I have is French toast and I like that. Does that count?"

Ellie laughed. She like this playful side of Jane. "Yes, it definitely counts."

Jane moved to within inches of her and Ellie's eyes widened. What was she doing? Up close and personal isn't what she does.

Leaning in, Jane lightly kissed Ellie's lips. "Can we do more of that after dinner? I saw a movie where a couple went out on a date and kissed afterward."

"What movie was it?"

Jane scrunched her face up. "I don't remember the name but I do remember the woman bending one knee in the air as they kissed." Jane pursed her lips. "Is that what I should do?"

Ellie laughed. "By all means you can do that, but it was more for an effect in the movie than anything else." *Unless of course if we were lying naked in bed then that bent knee might work.*

"Oh. Can I try it and see how it feels?"

"By all means."

Jane took a step closer, kissed Ellie's mouth, and then lost her balance.

Ellie grabbed her by the waist and pulled Jane closer. "If you're going to do that you have to hold on." She kissed Jane gently while suppressing the overwhelming need to go farther.

Jane stepped back. "Yes, holding on helps but I didn't find bending my knee made a difference."

Ellie grinned. "I like kissing you." She looked at her watch. "If we are going to be on time for our reservation, we'd better start getting ready."

"What should I wear? I have no frame of reference for eating at a fancy restaurant."

"Come on. I know exactly what you should wear."

†

Jane stepped out of her bedroom and the sight took Ellie's breath away. The hair was much shorter and the figure was a bit smaller but there was no doubt about it—Syd was standing in front of her. "You look beautiful," Ellie said.

The black cocktail dress revealed Jane's body perfectly and the heels showed off toned legs that seemed to go on forever. Ellie felt herself falling in love again.

"I know you said it before, but do you really think I'm beautiful," Jane whispered.

Ellie was immediately at her side stroking her cheek. "I've always thought you were beautiful. Tonight you are stunning."

Jane's forehead creased. "Always?"

Suddenly realizing what she'd said Ellie nodded. "Yes, from the first time I saw you at Salvation." There was no way she'd hurt Jane by letting her know she thought she was speaking to Syd. "What do you think of my get up?" she asked, trying to deflect her earlier faux pas.

"I like that color on you. It suits you."

Ellie looked down at her black silk suit with a forest green shell underneath. She stopped herself from blurting out 'remember when you helped me pick this out'. "I'm glad you like it. Are you ready to go?"

"Yes," Jane said before letting out a giddy laugh. "This is my first date." She moved toward Ellie and engulfed her in her arms. "Thank you for making me feel…important."

Closing her eyes, Ellie leaned into the hug. "You are important to me and always will be."

Ever since the CAT scan Jane had begun touching her and lately that had turned into hugs until this morning when they'd shared a kiss.

She's so much like Syd. Ellie smiled. She never passed up a chance to show me affection and how much she loved me...loves me. Ellie placed a soft kiss on Jane's hair and stepped back. "Are you ready to go?'

"Yes. I can't wait." Jane hooked her arm in Ellie's. "Let's go."

†

Jane felt like a princess as the maître d lead them to a secluded table and pulled out her seat. "Thank you."

"*De rien,*" the man responded. "Your server, Jean Paul, will be with you momentarily."

Jane's eyes took in the small, intimate restaurant. "This is amazing. I've never seen anything like it." Jane grinned. "Well, there's an understatement. Have we been here before?"

Ellie shook her head. "No. This is the first time for us both. Do you like it?"

"Oh, yes. Very much." Jane opened her menu. "It's all in French. Shouldn't there be prices?"

"You get a menu without prices so you order what you want and not by the price," Ellie explained.

"But how do I know what I want if I can't read what it is?"

"Easy. Three choices. The waiter can tell you, I can tell you, or I can order for us both."

Jane cocked her head. "You speak French?" Ellie nodded. "Did I speak French?"

"Yes and no. You didn't speak French but were fluent in Spanish."

"I would like it if you choose for me."

"Okay. what would you like beef, poultry, or seafood?"

Jane tried to remember all the meals she ate completely ruling out anything she'd had at Salvation for it paled in comparison to anything that Ellie cooked. "Beef, I think."

Ellie smiled. "Excellent. I know exactly what to order."

"Good evening, ladies. I am Jean Paul and will be serving you this evening. May I start you out with a drink."

Jane looked at Ellie and gave her an almost imperceptible nod. Not only was being on a date in a French restaurant out of her knowledge base but what to order was mystifying. Her inclination was ask for water but something told her that was not the right choice.

"A bottle of Château Margaux please."

"Excellent choice," Jean Paul said, before he left the table.

"Is that a wine?"

"Yes. Since we are having beef, a full bodied Bordeaux will pair with it nicely." Ellie's eyes widened. "Oh, I'm sorry. Would you prefer something else?"

"No. What you ordered is fine." Jane looked at Ellie intently before capturing her eyes and not releasing them. In that moment of clarity, she found herself drowning in emotions that were unfamiliar yet familiar. She sensed a deep and abiding connection, knowing this was what loving Ellie felt like. Ellie's hand on hers made her blink.

"Are you okay?" Ellie asked, her voice filled with concern. She withdrew her hand.

Jane smiled. "I can't believe that I am here with you on a date. I am having such a wonderful time. Thank you for not giving up on me." She bit her lower lip. "It can't be easy for you."

Ellie reached across the table and took Jane's hand. "In comparison to your recent experiences, mine are miniscule. I'll never give up on you, Jane."

"What about Syd? Have you given up on her?"

Ellie let go of Jane's hand and looked away. "I won't give up on either of you. You are one and the same," she whispered.

Jane felt the distance that her question caused and instantly regretted it. "So what have you decided for the meal."

"I think we will go for the three course meal. For starters we will have oxtail soup followed by Chateaubriand that is served with asparagus and new potatoes. Then for dessert I thought we'd have Galettes de Pérouges with cream and strawberries."

Jane grinned. "I haven't a clue what any of that is but I'm game."

"You'll love it. Generally oxtail soup has a rich brown broth with barley or vegetables and meat. Chateaubriand comes from the tenderloin of beef and is served in a wine sauce. The dessert is like a slice of pizza but only better."

Ellie smiled and tipped her head to one side. "I remember when I was in high school I went to France and visited the town of Pérouges which is a walled medieval town that sits on a hill overlooking a river valley. It was there that I first tasted the dessert. It was heavenly."

The look in Ellie's eyes told Jane that this was a fond memory. "Would you like to go back there some day?"

Ellie smiled wistfully. "Yes. Yes, I would."

"It sounds really interesting. Maybe we can go there together."

"I'd like that."

†

Jane pushed back from the table and put her hands over her tummy. "Wow. That was wonderful. I can't remember—" she grinned. "That's an understatement again—ever being so full yet completely satisfied. Thank you."

Ellie considered the comment taking in the look on Jane's face and her mind flitted back to having dinner with Syd. *That look was so familiar.* "I'm glad you've enjoyed yourself."

She watched as the waiter placed two small glasses of crème de menthe in front of them. She smiled at the man. "Thank you."

"Did you and Syd have dinners like this often?"

The question startled Ellie and she sipped on her drink as she considered an answer. "Sometimes. Why do you ask?"

Jane lifted a shoulder. "I'd like to know her better. Tell me about her please."

Ellie scrubbed her hand on her face. This wasn't remotely anything like the conversation she'd imagined they would have after dinner. "Are you sure you want me to tell you?"

"Yes." Jane's face became serious. "She and I are, after all, the same person. I'd like to get to know the other me."

Ellie sucked in a deep breath. "Okay. You and Syd are beautiful with a killer smile. Syd is brilliant. She holds advanced degrees in microbiology and molecular biology."

"I bet she loved her job."

"Yes, she did. The analytical part of discovering cures for diseases and pushing the boundaries of the research she did drew her in and kept her there."

Jane sipped her drink. "Yum. This is really good. I like the mint flavor." After resting the glass back on the table, she asked, "What did she do when she wasn't working?"

"Like you, she watched birds. You have that in common. Syd also gardened as a way to relax. Everything she grew always flourished." Ellie laughed. "She actually did an analysis of the soil and then added leaf mulch and other organic materials until the soil was perfect." Ellie smiled at the memory of watching Syd mix the soil and that reminded her of the look of pride when Syd presented her with a brilliantly red tomato.

"I saw the garden area." She took Ellie's hand. "It's been neglected. I'm sorry."

Ellie looked at the hand on hers. *That's Syd's hand.* "Jane, you can't remember so there is nothing for you to feel sorry about."

"If I could be Syd, I would," Jane whispered.

Turning her hand over, Ellie squeezed Jane's hand. "I like Jane just as you are."

"But...."

"But nothing." The waiter handed Ellie the check and she smiled at him. "Thank you." She pulled out her credit card and put it in the folder then looked at Jane. A tear trickled down Jane's cheek. "What's wrong?"

"I have nothing. I can't even pay for my part of the dinner."

"Oh, sweetheart, I invited you on a date and that means I pay." She saw another tear roll down the beautiful face across from her. "Just because you can't remember, doesn't mean you have nothing. You have a sizable bank account and the yellow truck in the garage belongs to you."

"But it's Syd's, not mine."

Ellie shook her head. "You are such a silly goose. It's only a name change. In here," she tapped her chest over her heart. "The woman then and now are the same to me."

Jane closed her eyes and sucked in a deep breath. "I want to have the surgery and find out what it is that they put in my head. That way…."

Ellie looked intently at Jane, waiting for her to continue.

"I want my life back. I want Syd back. If taking that thing out of my brain is the path to that happening, then I need to explore it."

"Take some time and make sure that is what you want to do. If you decide that it is right for you then I'll arrange with Dr. Stanley to do the procedure. He is excellent. Brain surgery is all he does and I'm pretty sure he wrote the book on it."

"I can think about it if you want me to but I'm certain that is what I want."

Ellie reached for Jane's hand again. "Come on. Let's go home."

"Is our date finished ?"

"Not by a long shot. I get to drive you home then kiss you at the door."

A grin curved Jane's lips. "I like the sound of that."

Chapter Sixteen

It had been a week since their date and Jane paced the floor of her bedroom. She was going to have lunch with her parents and the apprehension of going somewhere without Ellie was weighing heavily on her mind. Ellie made her feel safer than anyone else. Not that she didn't trust her folks to keep her out of harm's way. She did. There was something in Ellie's presence that calmed her like no one else. Even so she was looking forward to the lunch hoping they would shed more light on who Syd was.

†

Jane had just left with her parents and Ellie had to force herself to not follow them. As long as Addison was still in the wind, uneasiness was pervasive. In her heart she knew that Jane's parents would lay down their lives for their daughter but that still didn't stop the knot that twisted her belly when they left.

In two days Jane was scheduled for the procedure to remove the object just below the surface of her skull. Her colleague, Perry, had assured her that there would be little risk of injuring her brain but until he opened her up, he wouldn't know for sure. Ellie was miffed that he wouldn't allow her in the operating room—she understood the reasoning yet hated the thought of not being by Jane's side.

With each passing day, Ellie found herself falling for Jane and that both scared her and made her rejoice. Jane and Syd were one and the same. More of Syd Tanner became evident in Jane's mannerisms with each passing day. Ellie was certain that eventually Syd would return to her. The ringing phone startled her out of her musing.

"Hello… This is Dr. Scott… Hello, Dr. Easterday… Yes, Janet. How are you today?… That's great… Did you find something else?... And you placed the electrodes exactly where I said and nothing happened? That's bizarre… It sounds as though whatever its purpose is, it must work in conjunction with whatever is implanted in her brain… I agree… Yes…. The surgery is in two days so we will have the object then… You are?... When?... Okay, that sounds good. I'll see you on Wednesday then. Bye."

Ellie shook her head after ending the call. A shiver ran up her spine.

What is so important about Addison's device that would cause someone from the CID to be present when Jane has her surgery.

Something was telling her that Dr. Easterday was being less than forthright with her. Maybe she and Addison had joined forces to keep Jane from ever remembering. Ellie's mind was in a whirl of doubt and trepidation. She needed a contingency plan to thwart any move on anyone's part to sabotage Jane or her recovery.

Maybe I'm being paranoid but I'd like a backup plan just in case I'm right. As she paced the floor a plan began to formulate.

†

"I'm glad you decided to have lunch with us today, darling," Anita said, as they were perusing the menu. "I don't know if you remember or not but we used to come here every Sunday for brunch when you were around ten. The food is excellent. You used to love their macaroni and cheese and would always insist that you have it, even for breakfast."

Jane smiled at the woman. She was trying her best to fit into the role of daughter. It felt odd but at the same time she felt a connection to the man and woman who said they were her parents. She looked around the restaurant, trying to latch on to anything familiar. Nothing. *If only I could remember something.* "Sorry, I don't remember. Can you tell me what I was like as a child."

Anita covered her mouth as she let out a tiny cry. "I've been waiting for you to ask us that."

Craig patted his wife's arm and smiled at his daughter. "What do you want to know?"

Jane blew out a breath. "Everything."

Anita smiled. "My pregnancy with your brother was difficult and I spent five months in bed so I wouldn't miscarry. I already had five of them. After I had Mack, the doctors told me it was too dangerous to have another baby."

She saw the stricken look on Jane's face. "I almost died during delivery so when I found myself pregnant ten years later, I had to decide whether to go through with the pregnancy or not." Anita smiled at her daughter. "You are my greatest gift. The joy I felt when I first held you still gives me goose bumps."

"Right from the beginning we knew you were special," Craig added. "By the time you were three you were reading." He laughed. "Were you ever a handful. You were on the go every minute of the day and questions…you had a million. You made me laugh and filled my heart with so much love that at times I thought it would burst."

"Mack doted on you and he was your greatest protector." Anita smiled and patted Jane's hand. "When you disappeared, he came back from New Zealand and spent months with Ellie and alone trying to find you."

"Why didn't he come back when Ellie found me?" Jane's forehead furrowed. "I have a brother that I've never met."

"His wife Paula is about to have a baby and he can't get away right now." Anita's face brightened. "I know. We can have a video chat with him over the internet. That way you can see him for yourself."

Jane raked her fingers through her hair. "I'd like that."

"Consider it done," Craig said.

"Please tell me more."

"By the time you were twenty you had your first doctorate degree and were working on your second one," Craig said, pride evident in his voice.

"That's when I met Ellie."

Anita's eyes brightened. "You remember?"

Jane shook her head. "No. I just did the math and figured that was around the time we met." The disappointment on Anita's face was evident and Jane felt pangs of guilt. "Did you approve? I've read that same sex couples are often frowned upon."

"We fell in love with Ellie the first time you brought her home. It was easy to see that she brought out something in you that we'd never seen." Craig lifted a shoulder. "You glowed when you were around her so how could we possibly object."

"She made you happy and I could see that you made her happy." Anita laughed. "One time we all went camping together and Ellie was way out of her comfort zone but she soldiered on and made the best of it." She smiled fondly. "It was on that trip that you asked her to marry you."

Jane drew in a breath. "I wish I could remember that."

"You loved Ellie more than anything," Anita said softly. "And she feels the same way today."

A tear rolled down Jane's cheek. "What am I going to do if I never remember that love."

"Begin again." Craig touched his chest over his heart. "Whatever is lost in your brain is still in here. I've seen you with her and I can see the love you have for her even if you don't know you feel it."

"I have no frame of reference for what love is," Jane whispered.

"Sure you do. Love is what you feel for Ellie right now. We see the same glint in your eyes when she is near you, sweetheart. Your eyes follow her everywhere she goes." Anita squeezed Jane's hand. "It's that warm fuzzy feeling you have when you think of her. That does happen, doesn't it?"

Jane nodded and smiled. "So that is love?"

"Yes. The beginnings."

"Should I tell her?"

"Yes." Craig pushed back his chair. "Let's go find her."

Jane felt a shiver of excitement at seeing Ellie again.

✝

The door opened and Ellie blew out the breath she'd been holding. Jane was back and she was safe. "You're back. Did you have a nice time?" she asked, trying to slow down her rapidly beating heart.

Jane grinned broadly. "Yes. I learned so much about Syd." Without a wasted second she rushed into Ellie's arms. "I love you."

Ellie took a step back and looked into the eyes that reflected her blue shirt. "I love you, too. Do you remember?"

"No. My mother told me what love feels like and I know that is how I feel about you," Jane said softly. Arms encircled Jane's waist and pulled her close.

With a look of puzzlement Ellie's eyes found Anita's and when she nodded Ellie could feel her heart soar. "It's a start, baby. It's a start."

Mindless that her parents were still there, Jane pulled back. "Can we kiss now?"

Ellie chuckled. "Of course we can but I think we need to speak with your mom and dad, too." Ellie gave Jane a quick kiss. "Why don't we all go outside and I'll fix us something to drink."

"Why don't you help her," Anita said to her husband. "Jane and I'll set things up."

Once the two woman walked outside, Ellie turned to Craig. "That certainly was unexpected."

Craig laughed. "The Syd we knew was always that impulsive if it had anything to do with you."

"She's in there, I know it," Ellie said.

"I think so too. Once that thing is out of her head we might find out more."

"I wanted to talk to you about that."

"Why? Has she changed her mind?" Craig asked with concern.

Ellie shook her head. "No. I got a call from the forensic doctor who is looking into that machine they were using on her."

"And?"

"She wants to be here for the operation and I have a really bad feeling about that."

"Why?"

"It doesn't feel right. I think she might try to confiscate whatever it is and never let us know anything about it." Ellie wrapped her arms around her waist when she shivered. "It's all connected. I can feel it in my bones."

"So what can I do to help? You know that Anita and I plan on being there with you so it will be three against one."

"If she is there alone. What if she brings others with her…we won't stand a chance."

"I'll call Tom and see if he can be there or send some officers."

Ellie pulled glasses out of the cupboard and filled them with ice and lemonade. "That will make me breathe easier."

Craig picked up two glasses. "Is there some way you can get her to bring that machine with her?" he asked with a glint in his eyes.

"What do you have in mind?" Ellie picked up the other glasses and walked toward the door.

"Take it from her and have Tom's forensic people take a look at it."

Ellie shrugged. "Good idea. I'll see what I can do."

†

The night before her surgery, Jane snuggled close to Ellie as they watched an old movie called *The Enchanted Cottage*. Every so often she looked at Ellie and reveled in the emotions that played in her mind and body. "Do you think something like that can really happen," Jane asked as the movie ended.

Ellie kissed the top of Jane's head. "Yes. If your love is true then…it reminds me of a song, *The Look of Love*. True love cannot be denied and sees past the exterior and into a person's soul." She began humming the song. "I've found you so please don't go," she sang.

"Are those the words?"

"I don't think they are the real ones but it's something like that." Ellie pulled Jane close. "Would you like me to find it so you can hear it with all the words?"

Jane nuzzled further into Ellie's shoulder. "Yes, but not now. Can we just stay like this for a little while longer."

Ellie pulled Jane closer. "We can stay like this forever if you like."

"I know you want me to be Syd," Jane whispered. "And I wish I could remember for you."

With her finger cupped around Jane's chin, Ellie turned her head so that they were only inches apart. "I want you to be who you are, Jane. Yes, you look like Syd and there are many things that you do that are so much like her but you are Jane, the woman I am with…who I want to be with." Closing the gap, Ellie kissed Jane's lips softly.

Jane moaned and ran her tongue over Ellie's lips asking for and gaining entrance. Lost in the feeling of coming home, Jane whimpered when Ellie pulled away. "Did I do something wrong?"

"No, my love, you did everything right. Is this all right?"

"You mean, do I want to keep kissing you? Oh, yes, I do and I want more."

Ellie laid back on the couch, taking Jane with her before capturing her lips again.

The revelation that she loved Ellie had Jane scouring the internet about love and what people in love did. When Ellie's hand snaked under her shirt and gently brushed across her skin, Jane's body reacted pleasurably and everything she'd read suddenly made sense. Her body thrummed with anticipation of what was to come. She moaned into Ellie's mouth when a hand ran across her lower back. "God, Ellie. Please don't stop," she mumbled before letting her fingers take purchase of Ellie's skin.

Ellie stopped.

Jane lifted her head and searched Ellie's face. "What's the matter."

"Is this what you really want?" Ellie's voice was low and sensuous.

"Yes."

"Let's take this into the bedroom then."

Jane grinned and sat up. "I think that would be wonderful."

†

It was a dream come true for Ellie. She was naked, laying in the their bed, with Syd in her arms. She considered pinching herself to see if it was a dream. It wasn't. *But this is Jane and it's her first time.* The thought shook Ellie to her core. Patience. She would take great care in loving Jane and discovering all the ways to pleasure her. *I wonder if she will react the same as Syd?*

With feather light fingertips, Ellie explored all of Jane's body. "Is this okay?"

Jane let out a low moan. "Perfect. Don't stop."

Ellie's hands trembled as she cupped one of Jane's breasts. The shape, weight, and feel of it was exactly as she remembered but it was different. An unexplored territory that was calling her to adore what Jane was offering her. A virginal body begging for touches, caresses, and adoration.

She would not squander the gift and in doing so, she would show Jane just how much she loved her.

Jane reacted with a moan when Ellie first sucked a delicate nipple into her mouth. Ellie closed her eyes as she explored the familiar yet new body that her lips and fingers were paying homage to. Everywhere she touched, Jane leaned into the touch until she suddenly became demanding in what she wanted and needed. When Ellie dipped her fingers deep inside Jane's wetness, she felt the contractions and knew it wouldn't be long before Jane experienced her first orgasm.

Jane cried out as her back arched off the bed driving Ellie's fingers in deeper.

As the small spasms receded, Ellie gently removed her fingers and pulled Jane to her. "I love you, Jane," she whispered. To her surprise, Jane captured Ellie's lips before she began investigating every part of her body.

Drifting off to sleep with Jane nestled in her arms, Ellie felt the bubble of happiness she hadn't felt in what seemed like forever make its way to her heart.

Chapter Seventeen

Jane grasped Ellie's hand in the predawn as they entered the hospital. The night before had been spectacular, and the glimpse of what Syd and Ellie had, made her more determined to bring Syd back to life. She recalled Ellie's words, *I love you, Jane*, and knew that no matter what happened, Ellie would be by her side whether Syd returned or not. That gave her the courage to face the future, come what may. Having this operation was the first step toward what lay ahead of her.

"Are you okay?" The concern in Ellie's voice was unmistakable.

"Yes. As long as you are by my side, I'll always be okay." Jane turned and kissed Ellie's cheek. "Thank you for last night."

Ellie's lips curved. "I think I am the one who needs to thank *you*. Last night was magnificent because of you, Jane…only you."

The words touched Jane's heart. "I love you," she whispered as they approached the admittance desk.

"Here we go. Are you ready for this?"

"Yes. We've wasted enough time on me being afraid. It's time to go forward and not live in fear."

†

Ellie assisted Jane as she took off her clothes and put on the requisite hospital gown. Jane was lying on the bed with a look of apprehension on her face. Ellie took her hand. Words were not needed. All the tenderness and feelings they had for one another transmitted through their clasped hands.

The nurse that had showed them to the curtained area walked in and smiled. "Jane, I need to shave a part of your head." The tall slender woman looked at Ellie. "Will you step out, please?"

Ellie nodded only to feel Jane's grip tighten on her hand. "It's okay. I'll be right outside."

"I can't do this without you," Jane whispered.

Ellie looked at the nurse. "I'm her physician. Is it okay if I stand over there while you do that?" She pointed to the area at the foot of the bed.

"Sure."

As Ellie stood and watched a large circular portion of Jane's hair disappear, she recalled the previous night's passion. She was surprised at how willingly Jane had embraced their lovemaking. She expected Jane to be shy and passive but instead she was eager to take and give with the hunger of discovery. She resembled Syd somewhat but Jane was passionate in a way that was hers alone. Ellie's body still hummed with desire and need. Her eyes tracked to Jane and found her eyes fixed on her with love and trust.

"All done," the nurse said. She patted Jane's shoulder. "The anesthesiologist will be in shortly and so will Dr. Stanley." The woman nodded at Ellie as she pulled back the curtain before leaving.

Jane held out her hand. "Please, come here."

Ellie smiled. Holding Jane's hand wasn't all she wanted to do but this was neither the time or place.

"I want you to know," Jane said, her voice tremulous. "I want Syd back, not just for you but for me too. It's like I feel her in here." She touched her head. "Screaming at me to let her out. I recently realized that sometimes I feel like she is trying to claw her way out and that is when the pain tries to take control."

"I love who *you* are. A name is just that—a name—and doesn't define *you*. I love you, no matter what, and you can count on that forever."

"Good morning, ladies."

Ellie turned to see Perry Stanley standing by the curtain. "Are you ready for this, Jane?" he asked.

Jane looked at Ellie. "Yes. It is time to see what it is that they put inside my head."

The doctor smiled. "This should be a relatively short procedure."

"And I'll get whatever that thing is as soon as it is removed, right?" Ellie said.

"Yes. Just be sure you are scrubbed and ready when the time comes."

Ellie smiled. She'd spoken with Perry several times trying to impress upon him how important it was that the device or whatever it was shouldn't be in anyone else's hands but hers. There was no way she was going to let it conveniently get *lost*—it was far too valuable in solving the mystery of why Syd had been taken. "Thank you. I'll be ready and as I promise I will not interfere in what you're doing."

Perry nodded and then patted Jane's hand. "Any questions?"

Jane shook her head.

"All right then, I'll see you in the operating room."

Just as he left a tall, beautiful blonde woman wearing scrubs entered the room. "Hi, Jane, I'm Carrie Meadows and will be your nurse anesthetist today. I just need to ask you a few questions and check your airway."

"You do know that she has amnesia and probably won't remember much about earlier operations," Ellie said.

"Yes, I know that, Dr. Scott, and I understand that you can fill in the blanks for me."

Ellie smiled. She'd met the woman on several occasions and had requested that Carrie be the one to administer the anesthesia. "Yes, I can."

Once all the questions were answered, Carrie left the area. A nurse appeared. "We're ready for you, Jane."

Ellie leaned in and kissed Jane's forehead. "I'll be here waiting for you when you return," she whispered.

"And I will return, count on it."

After a brief kiss to Jane's lips, Ellie moved to the side and allowed the woman to roll the stretcher away. She closed her eyes and briefly prayed that Jane would indeed return to her. *Then we will start our new life together.*

✝

Ellie walked into the waiting room and was surprised by the number of people gathered there. She spotted Anita, Craig, and Tom and they in turn smiled. After holding up one finger, she quickly turned around and left the room. A few minutes later, Ellie walked back in and immediately went to her in-laws. "I have a private family waiting room we can go to. Follow me." She smiled at the police captain. "You too, Tom."

Before they left the room, a woman with mousy brown hair and thick glasses cleared her throat. "Dr. Scott?"

"Yes."

"I'm Janet Easterday from the CID."

Ellie gave the woman a curt smile. "Ah, yes, Dr. Easterday. With everything that is going on I forgot that you said you'd be here today." She looked at the other three. "Please give me a minute while I show my family to another room and I'll be with you after that."

"Certainly. I'll get myself some coffee while you're gone."

Ellie nodded and hurried the others down the corridor to a small room that had a couch, two chairs, a small table, along with a wall-mounted television. "This will be more comfortable than in that overcrowded room."

"Thank you, dear. Isn't that the woman you wanted Tom to watch?" Anita asked.

"Yes, she is."

Craig squeezed his wife's hand. "Then why are we in here?"

"I'm pretty sure she is worried about the number of people in the waiting room. The only time I've ever seen a room that crowded was when it involved someone from the police or fire department."

"You think someone is there to spy on us right?"

"Yes and I have a creepy feeling about that Easterday woman." Ellie looked at Tom. "Have you ever heard of a crime department forensics person coming to a hospital to retrieve evidence?"

Tom shook his head. "Not that I can recall. As I told you on Monday, I did speak with the agent in charge and he assured me she would bring that instrument with her."

"Shall we go see if she has it and then you can take possession of it?" Ellie shivered. "I might be paranoid where Jane is concerned but for some reason I don't trust that woman at all."

†

"Dr. Easterday," Ellie said while offering her hand. She had led the woman out into the corridor away from the crowded waiting room.

"Please call me Janet."

Ellie nodded. "Sorry about the delay, Janet. The waiting room was too crowded and I wanted my family to be comfortable." She turned to Tom. "This is Tom Barth."

Tom offered his hand. "Nice to meet you, doctor. I've spoken with Gerald Melendez and he assured me that you'd return the evidence that we confiscated at Salvation."

"Yes, he asked me to bring it to you and I do have it but I'll need to take it back with me so I can study it further after whatever is in Jane Doe's head is retrieved."

Tom, towering above the other woman, raised himself to his full six foot one. "You've had our evidence for several months now. Certainly in that time you've done all you can with it. This is our case and from now on we will run with it on the forensic side."

"Who do you think you are?" Janet's face took on a sour look. "You cannot just do that. This is my case."

After pushing back his jacket, Tom revealed his badge. "Sydney Tanner's case is mine. Has been since the day she disappeared. If you have a problem with that, Doctor, then I'd suggest you call your boss." He reached in his pocket. "I have his number if you need it."

"I know exactly who you are, Captain, so you don't need to flash your badge to intimidate me. I've worked with the police for more than twenty years so that badge doesn't scare me." Janet turned to Ellie. "Dr. Scott, I have been forthcoming with you on this case. How can you just stand by and let this man run roughshod over me?"

"Because you have been less than forthright with me, *Janet*." Ellie stepped into the doctor's space also. "Isn't that true?"

"Is there somewhere private we can go?" Janet asked. "There is something you need to know but..." she looked around. "I don't know who I can trust here."

Ellie raised her eyebrows. "Nor do I." She looked at her watch. "I can give you a short amount of time. I need to scrub in for surgery. Follow me."

Tom, Janet, and Ellie stood huddled together in a small alcove close to the operating suites.

"Okay, what do you have to say," Tom said.

"I had just figured out what that thing does when someone called me and told me that if I knew what was good for me, I'd give it back."

"Who was it?" Tom asked, a skeptical look on his face.

"All I know is that it was a man."

"What else did he say?" Tom looked at the woman. "For the record you should know that I'm not buying your story."

"It's the truth. I told him I don't deal with threats and he'd have to come up with a better explanation." Janet gulped in a breath. "He was silent for a long time then said it belonged to him and he would get it one way or another and told me I should cooperate."

"Did you?" Tom's eyes narrowed.

"Hell, no. There is no way I'd give it to him. It is too important to an ongoing case."

"What do you mean?" Ellie asked.

"I know what it does...or what it is used for."

"When we spoke last week you told me you didn't know what it was for."

"And that was the truth."

"Pull another one, lady. I don't know who you are working for but you tell them this…I will not allow any of you to get near Jane."

Janet help up a hand. "Hold on a moment. I'm not the enemy. I am a forensic analysis with a PHD in forensic psychology. I assure you, I am not working for anyone other than the state."

Tom, standing at Ellie's side, leaned in. "Let's listen to what she has to say. Who knows? It might help."

Ellie closed her eyes, then nodded. "Okay, why don't you tell me what you've found, Doctor."

"When you told me last week that you found something in Jane's head, it turned my investigation in a different direction. Once I came to what I thought was the right conclusion, I wanted to be here to speak with you face to face." She shook her head. "I didn't know who I could trust or if someone was listening in when we talked."

Although Ellie didn't believe the woman, her interest was piqued. "And what is it that you discovered?"

Janet looked around. "It's a nanobot controller," she said in a hushed tone. "I believe what is in Jane's head is a nanobot."

"That's experimental technology," Ellie said. "You're telling me my wife was being used as a guinea pig."

"I believe so but won't be certain until I can examine what they take out of her head."

Ellie looked at her watch. "I need to go." She pursed her lips. "Don't let her out of your sight, Okay, Tom?"

"I'll take her into the room with Craig and Anita."

"Good idea. I'll be back as soon as I can." Ellie looked at Janet. "You do know that if you are giving us a line of bullshit, we will find out and I'll personally see that no one will ever hire you again." With a stern look in the woman's direction, Ellie walked away.

✝

Ellie pushed open the door to the operating room and gasped at the sight of Jane's scalp pulled back. She then understood why family members should never be in an operating room. Sucking in a breath, she strode into the chilly room and waited by the door until the doctor waved her over. He dropped the tiniest object she'd ever seen into a specimen jar and handed it to her.

"There you go, Ellie. Not sure what it is but now you have it."

"Thanks, Perry. How's she doing?"

The man was smiling and his eyes crinkled in the corners.

"Great. I'll close her up and she should be in recovery within the hour."

"Thanks." Ellie resisted the urge to touch his arm and turned away. *Now to see if we can get some answers.* She looked at the miniscule object and a sense of disappointment filled her. *Surely something this small can't be responsible for what had happened to Jane's memory.*

✝

When Ellie entered the room where the others were waiting, she saw the black bag sitting on the table. "So you really did bring it," she said to Janet.

"Of course I did. Even before I was told to bring it, I was planning on it. This is much too valuable to leave behind." She eyed Ellie and pointed to the object in her hand. "Is that it?"

Ellie nodded. "Yes. Although it is so small I can't see how it will help."

"May I?" Janet held out her hand.

"Sure, why not?" With great reluctance she passed her the specimen jar.

"Nanobots are measured in micrometers. A hundred micrometers is about the size of one strand of hair."

Ellie pointed to the specimen. "That is much larger than that."

"Yes, it is. If I'm right, this is just the vessel that holds the nanobot. I believe that if we open it we will find a much smaller object that will be barely visible to the naked eye. First we need to hook up the machine and see how this," she held up the specimen jar. "Will react to it."

"Do you think it will?" Craig asked.

Janet nodded. "There's only one way to find out and that is to try it." She began to twist the top off the jar.

"Hold on a minute. Not so fast," Ellie said, grabbing the specimen jar out of the doctor's hand. "How do we know you are not trying to sabotage this by making it inoperable so we can't discover its true nature and help Jane recover her memory."

Janet just stood there shaking her head before pointing to the black bag on the table. "If I wanted to do that, I could have lost that at any time or rendered it inoperable." She ran her hand through her thick short brown hair and let out a sigh. "Look, I get it. Something terrible was done to your wife and right now you don't know who to trust. That's understandable. "I," she touched an index finger to her chest, "am not the enemy."

"You say that but I don't know it to be true," Ellie said through gritted teeth. "For all we know you are in cahoots with Addison."

"If I was, I assure you I wouldn't be here today and certainly wouldn't have brought you the evidence. I've spent twenty-one years on the job. I've had to work hard to be seen as a competent, intelligent woman. I have never tampered with evidence or sent out false reports." Her jaw torqued. "I take my job very seriously," she said with indignation in her voice.

Anita stood and took a few steps until she was able to put her arm around Ellie's waist. "I think we should trust her," she said. "We have to start somewhere."

Ellie turned her head and kissed Anita's hair. "You're right." She held out the container in Janet's direction. "Let's see what you can find out."

Janet nodded. "I really need a lab but I can do a rudimentary test that will give us an idea if the two are connected."

"Go for it," Ellie said.

"Captain, since you have the largest hands will you help me?"

"Certainly."

Janet handed Tom a pair of gloves and put a pair on herself. She unscrewed the jar. "Hold your hand out and I'll drop this into it. Then make a fist around it. Is that okay with you?"

Tom nodded. Once he'd made a fist he said, "What now."

"I'm going to place the probes from the machine around your hand."

"You're going to do what," Ellie interjected.

"Not to worry. I've done this to myself and it is harmless. My guess is that once it is all hooked up the captain here will feel the object in his hand move and that will tell us that they are synced somehow." Janet began placing the suction cups around Tom's hand. "Once we know the how, then we will know the why." She powered on the machine.

Tom's eyes bulged. "I can feel it wiggling around in my hand."

"Does it hurt?" Ellie asked.

"Somewhat," Tom replied.

"Okay. Let's see what happens when I do this." Janet twisted the dial and watched Tom. "Any reaction?"

"Yes. It is twitching more and is getting hotter. I get the feeling that whatever it is wants out."

Janet turned the machine off and removed the probes before opening the jar and holding it out. "Drop it in here please." Once the object was in the jar she sealed it.

"What can you tell us?" Craig asked.

"Well, this," she tapped the machine. "This definitely controls the nanobot. What the captain felt tells me that if the machine was turned up high enough it would probably make the bot move."

"Is that why she was in so much pain?" Ellie asked.

"If my suspicions are correct, I think someone was trying to access the bot from outside her room and when she succumbed to the pain is when that man came to see if he could control the bot locally."

"Are you saying that it wasn't working." Ellie looked at the woman with skepticism. "Were they trying to torture her?"

"Torture? No. More likely the bot has a specific purpose and their technology was flawed. You said for some time during her initial admittance she had no pain, just loss of memory. Right?"

"Yes, that was my understanding." Ellie said.

Janet shrugged. "We can assume that the bot was working at that time. It wasn't until later that she began experiencing debilitating pain. My guess is that is when the bot stopped working properly."

"Any idea on what its purpose was?" Craig asked.

"Considering that it was located in the medial temporal lobe of her brain, it's my guess that it was used for erasing or controlling her memory."

"That makes sense." Ellie turned when the door opened and saw the surgeon standing there. "Is she okay?" she asked with a touch of panic in her voice.

"Yes, she is doing fine. There were no complications and I expect a full recovery."

"Thank God," Anita said as she hugged her husband.

"They are taking her to recovery now," Perry said. "I'll meet you there and we can go into more detail about the procedure."

"Okay, thanks. I'll be there shortly."

†

Ellie stood by Jane's side waiting for the moment she'd open her eyes. Although she knew that would happen, trepidation and anxiety flowed through her body. When Jane let out a low moan the breath Ellie didn't know she'd been holding escaped from her mouth.

Jane's eyes popped open and she looked around the recovery room with a puzzled look on her face. Her eyes finally settled on Ellie."El, where am I?"

"You're in recovery. The operation was a success."

Wait a minute. She called me El.

Jane's forehead furrowed. "Ow, it hurts. Surgery? What surgery?"

A knot in her stomach tightened as Ellie digested the words. *Oh no, is her memory going again?* "Don't you remember?"

"No." Jane groaned again. "My head is killing me." Her hand went to her head. "What happened to me? Was I in an accident?"

"Remember? We took whatever was in your brain out. Please tell me you remember that, Jane?"

Jane's face contorted. "Who the hell is *Jane*?"

Ellie eyes widened. "Syd?" she asked tentatively. "Is that you?"

"Who else would I be?"

She bent and lightly hugged Syd. "You came back to me. I've missed you so much."

Syd held her hand on the bandage. "God, my head hurts."

"I'll have them get you something for that." Ellie blew out a breath.

"I came back from where?"

Ellie swallowed hard. "You've had amnesia. What is the last thing you remember?"

"Leaving work. Some asshole was in the backseat and put a gun to my head and made me drive out of town." Syd shook her head. "I remember him making me drive off the road. After that nothing."

"Would you like something to drink, Jane," a recovery room nurse entered and asked.

"Water." Syd looked at Ellie. "Who is Jane?"

Ellie lifted one shoulder and briefly closed her eyes. "You were. For a time."

Syd sucked in a breath before she yawned. "My brain is fuzzy."

"It won't last long. Why don't you try to close your eyes and sleep some."

Syd grabbed Ellie's arm. "I don't understand."

"I know, sweetheart. When you aren't so drugged, I'll explain everything. Get some rest. I'll be right here when you wake."

"Mom, Dad," Syd slurred, her eyes closing.

"They're in the waiting room. I'll go tell them you are awake. Okay?"

"K," Syd said before sleep captured her.

†

Ellie entered the waiting room with a beaming smile.

"Is she awake? Is she okay?" Anita asked anxiously.

"Yes, she is doing wonderfully."

Anita eyed her. "I know that look. What aren't you telling us?"

Ellie couldn't hold back the burst of happiness that was inside her. "Syd's back."

Chapter Eighteen

Syd walked into the familiar house and let out a sigh of happiness. After the horrific story of what she'd been through as Jane, she was glad to be back in the house where she knew love would surround her. The feeling of Ellie's arms around her waist with her body pressed against her back made her close her eyes, surrendering to the warmth spreading throughout her. She turned and pulled Ellie closer before kissing her softly. "Remember the last time we were here together?"

"You were begging me to come back to bed."

"Let's go to bed." Syd's voice was thick with desire. "I want you."

Ellie squeezed Syd closer. "I want you too." She kissed Syd's neck near her ear. "The doctor said we have to wait. I don't want to risk losing you again."

Syd disengaged and took a step back. "Did you make love with her?"

"You mean Jane?"

"Yes." Syd's voice trembled.

"I made love to you, Syd. The name might have been different but in my heart I knew it was you. From the first day I found you, I knew it was you."

"What was she like…this Jane person."

Ellie smiled and took Syd's hand, leading them to the couch. "She was very much like you. I often would see you in her mannerisms."

"But she wasn't me."

"Jane lacked your confidence, which was understandable after all she'd been through." Ellie laughed. "She only tolerated hamburgers. I took her to Archie's Hideaway, thinking it would spark a memory." Ellie shrugged. "Nothing happened and that was the first in a long line of disappointments trying to bring you back to me."

"At some point you must have decided you wanted to take her to bed." The pounding in her heart made Syd hold her breath.

"I thought I'd see if I could make you fall in love with me again and you did. We didn't share a bed until the night before the surgery. I was desperate to feel your body close to mine." Her eyes met Syd's. "I didn't know if I'd ever see you alive again. There was no way of predicting what would happen when they took that thing out of your brain." Tears trickled down Ellie's cheeks. "I don't think I could live if I lost you again. It was only a name, Syd. It was always you."

Syd couldn't hold back her tears any longer and clung to Ellie. Her lifeline. Her love. "God, how did we get here?" she sobbed. "Who did this to us?"

"I don't know, sweetheart, but we *will* find out."

"Right now, all I want is to be with you." Syd pulled back and gave Ellis a weak smile. "And a hamburger."

Ellie laughed. "What do you say I take my favorite girl out to Archie's."

Syd grinned. "I'd say let's go." She grabbed Ellie's hand. "Want me to drive?'

"No driving until we see the surgeon again in six weeks." Ellie picked up the key. "You ready to go, hot stuff?"

"I'll go with you anywhere." Syd grinned. "Think people will stare at me with this bandage on my head?"

Ellie laughed. "They will stare at you all right but not because of the that."

"What then?"

"Because you are so beautiful."

†

Cuddled in a love seat, Ellie rested her head on Syd's shoulder. Ever since Syd disappeared Ellie had kept all her mail paying any bills that needed attention but leaving the rest. She stored the mail in a clear plastic bin. During the weeks since the operation, Syd had made progress in sorting through it all and was now reading a scientific journal.

"I should start thinking about finding a job," Syd said.

"After you disappeared, Gary Linder came by for a visit and told me you'd always have a job at Paradyme." Ellie shrugged. "You said you weren't happy there that night before you disappeared."

Syd shook her head. "No I wasn't. Some of the trials they were running were faulty and after I spoke up about it they started ignoring my objections and giving me the cold shoulder telling me I didn't know what I was talking about. But I did." She rubbed the back of her neck. "I think I'd like to find somewhere else to work."

"Wasn't there some local company that kept trying to lure you into working for them?"

"Hilton Biologic. The problem with them was they were a startup and funding for research grants was minimal at best."

Ellie began rubbing Syd's neck in slow leisurely circles. "Maybe they have the funding now. I heard that after you disappeared some of the grants specific to your research were withdrawn."

"That's not unusual. That is probably why they want me back. To make them money." Syd smiled. "If you keep rubbing my neck like that I won't be able to promise I won't ravish you before we see the doctor tomorrow."

Ellie laughed and moved her hand before putting her head on Syd's shoulder again. "Just read your journal and I'll watch."

Syd turned her head slightly and kissed Ellie's forehead. "Tomorrow can't come soon enough."

"Good thing it is an early morning appointment because I have plans for you that involve a bath and a bed."

"Do you now. Maybe we should get a head start."

"Go back to your reading. You have loads to read and we have a long day ahead of us."

An hour later Ellie opened her eyes and yawned. "Sorry I fell asleep on you."

"Not a problem. I'm still reading." Syd held up the third journal she was skimming through.

Ellie gasped, grabbed the magazine, and jabbed at a picture. "Do you know who this man is?"

Syd shook her head. "No. He looks familiar but I don't know him. Why?"

"That's Addison."

"The man who did this to me?" Syd touched the bandage on head."

Ellie studied the picture. "Yes. That's him. I'd never forget his face."

Syd grasped the magazine from Ellie.

"It says here that his name is Jasper Beaucage and he is a doctor of neurobiology." She gazed at the picture and felt her body tense. "I know I've seen him but can't quite place him. We should call the CID and let them know we know Addison's real name."

"We will in a minute. First, turn around." Ellie's voice was soft.

"Why?"

"You're tensing up. Let me give you a shoulder massage so you won't get a headache. Remember you are supposed to stay calm and not get tense."

Syd snickered. "You think that will do the trick, do you?" Leaning in she kissed Ellie. "All it will do is make me hornier."

"Like that's a bad thing. Come on, turn around and let me try."

"Okay, but it isn't going to work." She melted into the strong fingers.

"That's it. Just relax and forget about everything else," Ellie cooed. When she felt Syd's neck muscles relax she smirked. "Oh, ye of little faith. It is working."

"It is also making me horny."

Ellie laughed. "You're not the only one."

†

Once the nurse removed the bandage, Perry came into the exam room and logged into the computer on the table. Pictures of Syd's recent brain scan appeared on the screen. "How are you feeling?" he asked Syd.

"Good. No headaches and I am remembering more each day."

"This is the latest scan and as you can see here," he pointed to an area with his pen. "The skull is completely healed."

Ellie leaned in and looked at the image. "That's remarkable."

"Yes, it is," Perry replied. "Have you found out any more about what that thing was doing other than blocking her memory?"

"No. The forensics team are certain that its purpose was to erase memory. Why that was done still remains a mystery."

"Can I get back to resuming my life, Doc? Can I be physical again and get worked up without worrying my head will explode?" Syd asked.

Ellie blushed when Syd turned her head to face her and wiggled her eyebrows as a lascivious grin curved her lips.

Thank God he was studying the screen and not looking at her.

The familiar rush that Syd caused in her body made her squeeze her legs together only to see her wife's grin broaden. She wondered if they would make it out of the parking garage. That thought sent another tingle surging through her body.

"There shouldn't be a problem resuming your normal activities as long as you gradually work back into them." Perry looked at Syd. "You're one lucky woman."

"How so?"

"I've been reading up on nanobot technology and luckily they didn't attach a charge to it because that would have fried your brain in seconds." The doctor pursed his lips. "Had I known that possibility at the time, I never would have done the surgery."

"And I would still be Jane," Syd said in a soft voice.

Ellie gasped. "I didn't know that was a possibility."

"Neither did we. That field is still in the developmental stage." The doctor shrugged. "We got lucky."

Syd grinned. "I got more than lucky. I got my memory and life back."

The doctor smiled and stood. "I want to see you back in a month for more scans just to make sure everything is as it should be. If for some reason you develop a headache—even a small one—call me immediately."

"Will do." Syd stood and held out her hand. "I thank you, Doctor Stanley." Syd smiled at Ellie. "Are you ready?"

The hungry desire in Syd's eyes was all Ellie saw as she stood. "Thanks, Perry," she said.

Perry stopped just as he got to the door. "You're most welcome," he said, before leaving the room.

Syd pulled Ellie to her and kissed her lightly. "Let's get out of here."

With that they rushed out of the exam room.

†

Once they were inside the car, Syd grinned."I'm glad you parked up here in this dark corner of the parking garage." When their lips met, a surge of emotion hit Syd and she moaned. "God, I want you so much."

The kiss intensified and fingers began their exploration of the body of the woman she'd always craved. Syd was oblivious to everything but Ellie's response to touches exactly as she remembered it always did. "I love you," she whispered before running her tongue across Ellie's ear.

Ellie pulled back and gulped down a swallow. "Not here. Not like this. I've waited too long to have a quick tumble in the front seat of a car."

"How fast can you get home?" Syd's voice was low and full of longing.

"We will be there before you know it." Ellie gave Syd one last kiss, straightened, and rolled her seat belt out.

Syd's hand never left Ellie's thigh as the car started and they began the journey home. "Hurry."

✝

Once inside the door, Syd pulled Ellie to her and began an exploration of the body she craved. She tore at Ellie's clothing, buttons popping and material tearing as she sought the flesh she'd dreamed of since she'd woken up as Syd. Every place she kissed or touched brought back memories and a longing she knew she'd always feel.

Ellie was pulling at Syd's clothes, seeking the familiar body that had eluded her for all those months. Her need to feel Syd's body close was overwhelming.

Somehow they managed to make it to the bedroom, leaving a trail of tattered clothes behind them. Their lovemaking was passionate and aggressive, neither willing to take time for foreplay. The need and the drive was all they knew until they screamed out in pleasure.

Laying on her back, with Ellie's head on her shoulder and one leg across her legs, Syd sighed. "My God, that was exactly how I've wanted you since I opened my eyes in the hospital. Even though I don't remember those months I was gone, in here," she touched the center of her left breast, "I know I always dreamed of you."

"None of that matters," Ellie whispered. "You returned to me and are here now. That's what matters. I will never let you go again, even if it means I have to quit my job and be with you twenty-four seven."

"I wish I could remember why it all happened."

Ellie rolled on top of Syd. "We have more pressing matters than that right now." She kissed Syd's lips before running her tongue along them seeking entrance. When her mouth opened, Ellie began the dance again.

Chapter Nineteen

Ellie woke with a smile until she saw Syd curled in a fetal position. She had hoped that once they made love, Syd would sleep in a more comfortable position. It wasn't the way Syd slept before she'd disappeared. Far from it. Before that, Syd would be spread out on the bed with her body draped over Ellie's. Ever since Syd returned, Ellie surmised that she slept that way because of a subconscious reaction to what had happened to her before and during her time at Salvation. The key to that puzzle was still elusive.

"Good morning, beautiful." The smile in Syd's voice was evident. "What's got you frowning?"

Ellie tried to smile. "It's nothing."

Syd sat up and put her arms around Ellie's naked body. "Hey. It's me and we haven't lied to one another in all these years so let's not start now. What's going on?"

"You were sleeping."

"Yeah. I do that every night. So what about me sleeping has got you in a funk?" Her arms tightened around Ellie. "Out with it."

"Ever since you got your memory back you've been sleeping in a fetal position and that has me worried."

"Why?"

"I think someone must have tortured you before Salvation and you are repressing it."

Syd kissed Ellie's cheek. "Funny you should say that because I keep having flashbacks of lying naked on a concrete floor."

Ellie's hand went to her mouth. "Oh, my God, no. Why didn't you tell me?"

"Because I don't have anything else. It wasn't a full blown memory but it's something that I can almost grasp but it's just out of reach. Until I know it all, I didn't want to worry you with it."

"You're right. I would have worried but I also would have tried to help you through it." Ellie turned in Syd's arms. "Can we try something."

Syd grinned and waggled her eyebrows. "You can try anything you want with me."

"Not that, silly." Ellie grinned too. "But later, after we talk, I'd like you to rock my world again." Her grin broadened. "And again."

"You're on. I'm famished and since I can't ravish you yet, let's go have some coffee and those wonderful cinnamon scones you made. You can tell me all about what you want to try."

"Sounds like a plan." Ellie hugged Syd close and gently kissed her lips. "That's my promise of what's to come."

†

Syd watched as Ellie raised her cup and took a sip of coffee. It was a scene that she'd memorized ever since the first day she saw Ellie at Starbucks drinking coffee and reading a book. Later, after she worked up the nerve to approach the beautiful woman, she'd learned that Ellie wasn't reading *War and Peace* but a medical book. Since then, watching Ellie sip coffee always invoked fond memories.

"So, are you going to tell me what it is?"

Startled, Ellie looked up and set her coffee cup down on the table with an audible clink. "If you don't want to do it, you don't have to." She picked up a scone and dunked it in her coffee, refusing to look up.

Syd reached and took her wife's hand. "Don't you know that I'll do anything so we can get to the bottom of this and get back to our lives."

Ellie nodded then looked into Syd's eyes. "Yes. I know that."

"Out with it then."

"Remember when I left that morning?"

Syd lifted her lips with a half a smile. "Like it was a few weeks ago." She chuckled. "Hey, it was a few weeks ago for me."

"Very funny. I'm trying to be serious here."

"I know. I'm sorry. Please continue."

"Can you go back to that day and tell me everything you remember?"

"Sure. I'll try."

"You were standing at the door and you took my breath away. I wanted you so much." She shivered. "I can still feel myself throbbing after you left. I tried to go back to sleep but I was so wound up that every time I closed my eyes there you were. Around eight I finally gave up trying to sleep and took a shower." Syd closed her eyes. "I was listening to the news while I was having my coffee and found we were in for a sunny day so I decided to change my appointment and see if I could get my truck detailed then."

"I remember taking my notes on my latest project with me to read while I waited for the detailing. The medicine I was developing showed a serious adverse reaction in our tests. I remember feeling agitated because Gary refused to consider stopping the tests and for me it was the only ethical thing to do until we figured out a solution."

She took a moment to gather her thoughts. "After that I started to go to the grocery store because I was hungry for one of those awful frozen pizzas in a box you never let me have but I didn't go there. Instead I stopped by Twin Pizza and bought two slices and took those home.

"By the time I finished the pizza, it was time to get ready for work. I wasn't looking forward to it. I was determined to argue my point with Gary and stop all testing no matter what. The grant for the testing was mine and if I withdrew, it would damage the company's reputation but I couldn't let it go forward like it was.

"When I got there, I was frustrated to find that Gary was in a behind closed door meeting. I left several messages for him to get back to me and that it was urgent."

Syd stopped for a minute. "Oh, yeah, I spoke to my folks and texted you earlier in the evening. Anyway, it was an hour before my shift was over and Gary was still not responding to me so I went to his office and walked in. He was sitting at his desk talking to another man and I remember they were both startled." Syd snapped her fingers. "That's where I saw that man in the magazine. He was the one Gary was speaking with."

Ellie's eyes widened.

"I'm sure it was him. Gary got up and came up to me and asked me to leave. I told him not until he heard me out, otherwise I was going to start the procedure to stop the grant. He told me he understood my hesitation and he would speak with me the next day. He told me to come to his office as soon as I arrived.

"When I left the building about an hour later and got in my truck, some man sitting in the backseat stuck a gun in my neck and told me to unhook my seatbelt and drive. I remember thinking about you and how I wouldn't get a chance to say goodbye. I knew he was going to kill me. I offered him money, the keys to the truck, anything he wanted, but all he did was jab the gun in my neck harder. He told me to turn off the road and to watch the odometer and when I'd gone five tenths of a mile to make a sharp left and hit the gas." She shrugged. "I didn't have a choice and I thought if I did what he said, maybe he wouldn't kill me. That's when my world caved in on me. My truck was sailing down an incline.

"I don't remember much after that until I woke up and saw your face."

"Tell me about the man," Ellie said.

Syd quivered. "All I remember is his voice. It was soft yet angry with a touch of malevolence that terrified me." She wrapped her arms around her waist. "I'd never heard anything like it. The way he phrased his words it was almost enticing, making me want to do whatever he said. But all I could think of was not seeing you again."

"Could you see him in the rearview mirror?'

"No. No, he was in shadow."

"Anything else? Like, could you smell him? Or get an idea of his size?"

Syd thought for a minute then shook her head. "From the way he was sitting I think he was around six foot cause his head was almost touching the ceiling. I know when my dad sits in the back seat his head is in the same position."

"Good. Keep it going."

"Old Spice. I smelled Old Spice."

Ellie hugged Syd. "You're doing great. Now I want you to think about that thing you told me about lying on the concrete naked. Can you tell me any more about it?"

Syd rubbed her face then ran her fingers through the hair that was still growing out. "I don't know, it is just a blur."

With the greatest of care, Ellie pulled Syd closer before kissing her. "Enough for now. What do you say we take a nap."

"I'd like that." Syd snuggled into Ellie's shoulder and yawned. "I don't think I can do anything but go to sleep. I'm sorry but once I reenergize, look out."

"First you will sleep," Ellie said as she wrapped her arm around Syd's waist when they walked up the stairs. "Then I am going to take advantage of you so completely that you will be begging me for more."

Syd smiled. "I like the sound of that," she said crawling under the covers. She yawned again and closed her eyes.

†

"No don't do this," Syd cried out, before opening her eyes. Ellie was there looking at her with concerned eyes while her gentle fingers were stroking her hair. "Are you real?" Syd asked.

"Of course I am. You were having a bad dream, that's all."

"No. It was more than that. I know what happened and I know one of the people responsible."

"Seriously?"

Syd nodded.

"Tell me."

"They took me because I wanted to stop the trials. The potential sales of the drug were huge. All that was needed was a delivery system that would go directly to the pancreas where it would change the molecular structure giving the pancreas a kick start. It was working great until I saw the stats that indicated there was a twenty-five percent increase in the incidence of pancreatic cancer. I had to stop it. I had no choice. They didn't see it that way."

"Why go through this elaborate ruse? Why didn't they just kill you?"

Syd felt Ellie shiver when she said the words. "Murdering me was never part of their plan. Instead they tried to erase my memory with that *bot* thing. I now remember a conversation with Gary about using a nanobot for the delivery system but the technology was so far off and it looked like at the time that the drug was going to work. We had opted for a surgical implant."

Ellie rubbed the corner of her mouth with the tips of her fingers. "We know the CID is looking for Addison—Jasper Beaucage, I mean—but he has disappeared too. You said you know one of the people who did this to you. What is the name?"

"Carly Madison." Syd shook her head. "She was not only a co-worker but I thought a friend."

"She was at your memorial service crying her eyes out. She even came up to me and said how sorry she was. I remember wondering if she had a crush on you since her apology was so fraught with sorrow." Ellie tapped her lips. "She may be the weak link. Why don't we call Captain Barth and maybe he can bring her in for questioning."

"Good idea." Syd looked away and let out a small sob. "First I need to tell you something else I remembered."

Ellie frowned. "Look at me." Syd wouldn't make eye contact. "Whatever it is we can work it out together." She grasped Syd's chin and lifted her head. "Please tell me."

Syd blew out a breath and nibbled on her lower lip. She knew Ellie needed to know everything but she didn't have any solid proof and why open a can of worms if she didn't need to. Yet the look of trust and love on Ellie's face gave her the courage to speak. "I may have been raped," she whispered then looked away.

"What makes you think that?" Ellie asked as she gently turned Syd's head so their eyes met.

"When I woke up, I was in some sort of dark room naked and with my hands and ankles bound." Syd sucked in a breath and let it out slowly. "I could feel that my body was beaten and I was aware that the area between my thighs was bruised." She shrugged. "What else could it be."

"Part of their torture," Ellie said softly. "If you were raped, you would have known it," Ellie tapped the skin over Syd's heart. "You'd know it in here." She kissed Syd's lips lightly. "Until you tell me you know it for a fact, then I choose not to believe it and so should you."

Syd felt her body relax. Ellie was right. It was a non-issue and that was what she'd choose to believe. But if they found Carly, she would make sure the police asked her if it happened.

†

"I'll meet you out in the garage," Ellie said. They had planned a day out to enjoy the beautiful spring.

"Give me a minute to go to the bathroom."

"Okay. Hey, can you bring the sun screen when you come?"

"Sure."

226

Ellie walked into the garage and her left fingers touched the door opener. Just as she got to the driver's side hands wrapped around her neck.

"No!" she screamed as she tried to get away. In the side mirror, all she could see was white hair. *Addison.* Frantically she felt for her car keys and started pressing buttons until the car's alarm began to blare. She bent her arm and with all her might jammed it into the man's ribs.

"Bitch," he shouted. "You ruined me and you're going to pay."

The hands tightened around her neck and Ellie began kicking backward hoping to catch him in the knee. Suddenly there was a commotion and she heard Syd's voice. "Let her go."

"Get off me, bitch."

Through the car's side mirror she saw Syd on the man's back punching him about his head. His hand loosened enough for Ellie to fish her phone out of her pocket and pressed the emergency button. "Help," she screamed when she heard, *what's your emergency.* The man grabbed the phone and threw it on the concrete floor. She saw Syd's punches making contact and Addison let go of her for a minute. That was her chance to turn and raise her knee hitting his groin with all her might.

Addison doubled but managed to grab Ellie's leg and pull her to the ground with him. She was face to face with the man as she mustered all her strength and jammed a key into his eye. He screamed in pain and rolled onto his side.

Syd gave him a swift kick in the ribs just as the sound of sirens filled the air. "Are you okay," Syd asked as she crawled over the man."

Ellie rubbed her neck. "Yeah, I'm good. How about you? Did he hurt you?"

"No." Syd sucked in a breath. "We make a good team, don't we?" she said, as two policemen with guns drawn approached them.

"This man attacked me, officers. He was involved in a kidnapping and there is a warrant out for his arrest." Ellie sighed. *Would this ever end?*

†

Although Carly Madison had left Paradyme six months earlier, it didn't take the police long to find her. According to Captain Barth, the woman admitted her involvement in the kidnapping and subsequent torture of Sydney Tanner and eagerly gave up the others.

Syd's knee beat a steady tap as she waited for Tom Barth to come into the interview room. She purposely made the appointment with the captain for a time she knew Ellie would be at work. Of course, Ellie said she'd take time off to be with her but Syd convinced her she'd be okay alone. There were questions she needed to ask and didn't want Ellie to hear the answers. Ellie was with her when she gave the captain her initial statement about what had happened. Now it was just a matter of her signing the statement. By doing that she would, in effect, put an end to the nightmare her life had been for almost two years. The door opened and she felt her heart skip several beats.

"Dr. Tanner, thank you for coming in. I have your statement for you to check. If there are no additions or corrections, you can sign it and we will be done here."

Syd took the paper and read through it. "It seems in order to me. Is it true that everyone but Gary Linder pleaded guilty?"

"Yes, it is. Both Carly Madison and Maya Rojas turned state's witness and we have a solid case against both Gary Linder and Jasper Beaucage."

"Should I be worried about Beaucage? I know he's in custody, but he seems to be able to worm his way out of trouble."

Tom shook his head. "No, I don't think so. Now that we have him, we won't let him get away this time. We have compelling evidence against him and since he skipped out on bail before, I can't see any judge granting him bail."

Syd chewed on her lip before asking, "Did you find out whether I was raped or not?"

"According to Ms. Madison, you were only beaten."

"How do we know that is the truth?"

"According to everyone involved, she was the only one who had any contact with you before they transferred you to Salvation. They thought that since you worked together, you would be more receptive to her. She didn't start beating you until several days later when you still refused to cooperate. They knew about your relationship with Ellie and they ordered her to repeatedly kick you in the groin telling you that she would never want you again "

Syd couldn't believe what she was hearing. "She's the one who beat me?"

"Yes. She said they made her do it to show her loyalty. That they would always watch her so she had to do everything she could to make you concede. At one point she was afraid they'd kill you and she didn't want any part of that so she did what they told her to do."

"I thought she was my friend," Syd whispered.

"There was big money behind this and she was paid very well to turn against you."

"Yet she will go free because she is testifying against them?"

"No. She will have to serve a lengthy jail term for her involvement."

"What about Dr. Rojas?"

"She will not serve any time for it appears she was duped into what happened but she has lost her medical license and was ordered to pay a hefty fine."

"So it's over then?"

"Yes." He smiled.

Syd nodded as she stood and extended her hand. "Thank you for everything. I understand you were on this from the start and I appreciate all you've done on my family's behalf."

"You're welcome. It is always a good day when we put away the bad guys and save someone's life."

"Yes, it is." Syd left the room with a lighter heart than when she'd entered.

Once in the hallway she pulled out her phone and texted Ellie, who was at work.

It is done and now we can begin our lives again.

She would wait until they were together to tell her everything. Her phone binged and she looked at Ellie's reply.

You will always be my beginning and my end.

Epilogue

The day was bright and sunny as Syd and Ellie walked along the beach hand in hand. It was more than a year since they'd last been there and so much had happened that it seemed more like an eternity. It was their eleventh anniversary and once again they were headed for the narrow path that lead up and away from the beach. This time the sunset was hours away but they had a mission.

The hundred yard climb up the side of the hill wasn't as taxing as Syd remembered. Once she'd been cleared by Dr. Stanley, she'd gone back to running every day. The events of the last year had changed her priorities in life. The most important one—Ellie.

She still hadn't found a job that she felt comfortable doing but had several interviews the next week and they sounded interesting. She liked being there when Ellie came home from work. Although she had always enjoyed working the night shift, since it wasn't as noisy and she could concentrate without being disturbed, she liked being with Ellie more. Any job she took would be the same hours that Ellie worked.

Once they made it to the large flat rock they always sat on, Syd took Ellie in her arms and kissed her soundly. "Happy anniversary, my love." She tightened her hold. "I love you more than I thought possible. With each day my love for you grows and being here with you fills me with joy."

Ellie kissed Syd before moving away and spreading a blanket on the rock. "Come lay with me," she said in a low voice. "I want to make love to you."

Syd lowered them both to the blanket. "You know there's a good chance someone might see us."

"I don't care." Ellie pulled Syd close and their lips met. Her kiss was full of promise as her tongue asked for and was granted entrance. She never grew tired of the game Syd played by hiding her tongue and making Ellie search for it. It was such a turn on. After moaning her pleasure, Ellie lifted her body off Syd so she could pull the t-shirt off and unzip Syd's shorts. No underwear. Perfect. It took Ellie less than a minute to take her clothes off and soon their naked bodies were one.

They had made love that morning yet it didn't quench their desire to love again. This time it would be slow and gentle until they were both ready to explode.

Syd ran her fingertips down Ellie's back and beyond until they reached her thighs. She growled softly and flipped them. Her eyes feasted on the naked body below her. The creamy white breast with brown nipples immediately caught her attention and she pinched them both before rolling them between her fingers. Her lips were on Ellie's and they kissed passionately.

Ellie melted into the sensations that were bombarding her body. She wanted to taste Syd's lips and drown in all that was her lover. The tantalizing body above her was begging to be touched and she reached out mirroring what Syd's fingers were doing as they caressed her body.

Syd was losing her breath with every touch of Ellie's fingers. She knew deep within her soul that she was home.

Her fingers delved into the velvet moisture and she felt that Ellie was as ready for her as she was for her wife. When Ellie entered her, she moaned in delight and tightened around the fingers that she knew would bring her to release.

In a lifetime of harmony, Syd and Ellie found mutual release as their passionate voices echoed all around them affirming their undying love.

Syd and Ellie huddled together with the blanket wrapped around them as the breeze off the ocean found them.

"It won't be long now," Syd whispered.

"I take the fact that we've always seen the flash on this day as a sign that we will always find our way here for the rest of our lives."

Syd grinned. "Do you really think we can make it up here when we are in our eighties?"

"If I have to pinch your butt the whole way, we will make it. This is our place and always will be."

"I can't believe how lucky I am," Syd said wistfully. "I think I dreamed of you all my life and when I saw you in that coffee shop I knew you were the one. I'll never forget that look in your eyes when I first said hello."

Ellie closed her eyes and smiled. "Did you know you melted my heart with that one word." She caressed Syd's cheek. "We've been through a lot this last year and it only proves that nothing will ever keep us apart."

"I love you so much," Syd kissed Ellie. The both turned and watched the sun set out over the ocean and just as it dipped below the horizon they saw not one but two green flashes.

About the Author

Erin O'Reilly

Erin O'Reilly: An accomplished author with several published works, including her newest Amazon bestseller *If I Were A Boy* and Sapphic Readers Award winner *Deception* to name but two. She also from time to time collaborates with other authors on very successful series.

Her focus as a writer is to develop strong characters that make a dramatic impact on her storylines.

Currently residing in Texas, she is also the technical Director and CEO of Affinity eBook Press.

Contact Erin at erinoreilly@affinityebooks.com

Other Books from Affinity eBook Press

Terminal Event—Ali Spooner Tally Rainwater was born with the gift of second sight. A near fatal accident, at age twelve, brings her visions to her more clearly. As she matures, a spirit enters her visions to guide her in using her gift. When Tally uses her gift to locate the body of a murdered teen, she realizes her gift is to help lost souls find their peace. When it's discovered a serial killer murdered the teen, the FBI is involved. Blaire "Spooky" Cooper is the Agent in Charge assigned to the case, and a task force of local detectives and FBI forms to track the killer. Together with the team, Tally helps them piece together the puzzle of murders spanning twenty years throughout the Deep South.

Arc Over Time—Jen Silver Dr Kathryn Moss has job offers flowing in after her exciting archaeological discoveries at Starling Hill the previous year. Now she has choices to make that could jeopardise her relationship with Denise Sullivan, the fiery journalist, who has become her lover. For Denise the choice seems obvious. She thinks they have moved beyond the casual sex stage to something more like a true relationship. However, she's not sure how to handle Kathryn's continuing infatuation with Ellie Winters. Ellie's new career as a promising artist proves to be a catalyst for the simmering tensions in relations between her wife Robin, Kathryn, and Denise. Will Denise persevere in her pursuit of the reluctant professor? Does Ellie have anything to fear from Kathryn's fascination with her art, or is there another motive behind the professor's obsessive interest? This wonderful romantic continuation with the characters from *Starting Over* ties up loose ends. But the question is—does everyone have a happy ending? A must read.

Presence—Charlene Neal After catching her husband red-handed in bed with his secretary, Kayleigh Gibbs takes her daughter and her Jeep and flees across the country. She opens up her own veterinarian practice, and they move into an old, secluded farmhouse in Hoekwil, South Africa. At her best friend's housewarming party Kayleigh meets the beautiful and enchanting Rebecca Steward. Rebecca is instantly drawn to Kayleigh, but is still recovering from a breakup—her girlfriend left her for a man. She's afraid of a repeat performance with Kayleigh, and won't pursue a romantic relationship with her, preferring instead to develop a platonic friendship. When odd, inexplicable things start happening on the farmhouse, a terrified Kayleigh turns to Rebecca for comfort, only to find herself developing unexplainable feelings for her new friend. Rebecca, despite her best intentions, is falling in love with Kayleigh. But when Rebecca moves in with Kayleigh to help her get to the bottom of the haunting, she finds more than she bargained for. Can Rebecca and Kayleigh overcome ghosts from the past and their own insecurities, or will a presence from the past tear them apart?

A Walk Away—Lacey Schmidt   Kat and Rand's daily worlds are 2,100 miles apart, but something about their meeting on the magical shores of the nation's oldest national park east of the Mississippi sparks questions that neither woman can just walk away without answering. Sometimes chance brings you to the right person to help you resolve some of your baggage, and you learn to like yourself a little more. Kat and Rand are smart enough to recognize this chance in each other, but they also find that there is a catch to every opportunity—walking toward something is always walking away from something else.

Love Forever, Live Forever—Annette Mori   No one forgets their first love. For Nicky, that's Sara, who abruptly disappears one day, leaving only a cryptic letter. That day scarred her soul. When the pain starts to diminish, Nicky begins to get her life back on track until it is derailed once again by an unimaginable twist. Changed forever, Nicky becomes a careless, womanizing nomad known as the Little Wild One, until she meets Annie. Thirteen years later, Nicky's finally settled and happy. Fate intervenes and puts her directly back into the path of her first love, Sara, and the corresponding events send her into a tailspin. Now she must decide—who will be the person she ends up living with and loving forever?

Possessing Morgan—Erica Lawson   New York City, in the height of summer. Crime seems to have taken a holiday, and Detective Morgan O'Callaghan is bored, bored, bored. Paperwork is mating and multiplying on her desk, and even a jaywalker is starting to look good. Anything to get her out from behind her desk! Enter Andrea Worthington, Charleston socialite and all-around rich girl, right down to the wealthy fiancé. She's also the new Assistant District Attorney assigned to Morgan's precinct. Their first meeting is like two freight trains crashing head on. Then a high profile, career make-or-break murder case throws them together again. The investigation has barely begun when Andrea becomes the target of a nearly fatal hit-and-run. But was it really aimed at her? Can she and Morgan find the common ground they need to solve the case and stop the attacks, or are the gaps just too wide to bridge?

Twenty-three Miles—Renee MacKenzie Talia Lisher has a long family history of lying, about anything and everything. With her father dead, and her mom gone on a quest to start a new life, Talia struggles to keep in touch with her only remaining family, her incarcerated brother. When Talia sets her sights on Officer Shay Eliot, she vows to stop lying. She starts watching Shay, waiting for just the right circumstances and amount of courage to talk to her. Talia might be watching Shay, but someone in a dark van is watching Talia. Is the mystery driver a dangerous part of her family's past, or is it all just a coincidence? Shay Eliot has left the police force because of what she perceives as a hostile work environment. When a brutal double-murder on the 23-mile-long Colonial Parkway puts the FBI's magnifying glass squarely on her, her alibi comes from an unlikely source – a young woman who has been stalking her. Shay wants to keep her distance from Talia, but once she gets to know the younger woman she can't keep feelings from developing. This is a story about community, and how it comes together in dangerous and devastating times. When you don't know who to trust, you better have friends who will rally around you. Will Talia and Shay find the answers they need to the mystery of the murders on the parkway, or will justice be elusive? Will they survive their quest for the truth?

Confined Spaces—Renee MacKenzie Andie Waters spends her days pulling waste samples for environmental testing and at night, she tends bar at The Cave, a popular hangout for straights in a small Georgia town. Serial monogamy has grown stale for her, so she's content working to pay off her debts and hanging out with her old hound dog. Or so she thinks, until a beautiful lesbian drops by The Cave. Andie suspects her involvement with the woman will be only temporary. Little does she know no part of her life will be left untouched. Kara Travis likewise anticipates nothing more than a brief fling upon meeting Andie, especially given her reputation as both a personal ice princess and a corporate hatchet wielder for Royal Environmental. What luck to find a hot lesbian bartender in nowhere rural Georgia. Andie and Kara spend a passionate weekend together and find that their notions of no strings attached are far from accurate. Their supposed short-term ideal diversion of a commitment-free romp hits a major complication when they come face-to-face with one another at Royal Environmental's offices Monday morning. While carrying out her duties, Kara discovers crimes being committed by and against Royal Environmental employees. Will Kara be forced to shut down the Georgia Division of the company? If she does, Andie will lose her job. Worse yet, Kara may lose Andie before she's really even sure she's got her. Corporate politics, complicated romance, and long distances conspire to keep Andie and Kara all boxed in. Can love triumph despite the Confined Spaces?

Reece's Star—TJ Vertigo Reece Corbett watches over the dancers in her gentleman's club with the blue, razor sharp eyes of The Animal. Few know that resting comfortably in her office is her newest love, a tiny MinPin named Smudge. What happened to The Animal, known for her rapacious appetite for women and danger? Faith Ashford is what happened to The Animal. Faith and Reece have been together a while now and they have settled into something resembling domestic bliss. This bliss alarms Reece. It's one thing for Faith to see her softer side, that's vulnerability enough, but to let her friends see it…no. Not the best plan. Under Faith's guiding, loving hand, will Reece successfully traverse the rocky road of emotion and embrace the positive changes in her life? Or will she panic and be unable to control that Animal part of herself? Will she take that next step to declare herself fully capable of love and devotion? This third installment in the popular series that began with *Private Dancer* continues the passionate and often hilarious romance of Reece and Faith as they both grow in love and in trust.

Flight—Renee Mackenzie It's 1983 and Kate Hunter is a student at a small, private college in Virginia. When Lana coaxes her onto the back of her beat-up scooter one night, Kate's education starts to encompass more than just her pre-vet studies. Kate has always done as expected of her, so when she starts staying away from home on weekends to spend time with her new lover it's way out of character for her. Lana is secretive, but Kate accepts things as they are and gives Lana her space. When she feels the sting of betrayal, will she be able to continue giving Lana her privacy? Kate's sister April is a high school student playing with fire as she parties with her older boyfriend, Boyd. After finding someone overdosed the morning after a big party, April grows weary of all the drugs and alcohol. Will she be able to convince Boyd that they should slow down? Will she be able to pull it together before it's too late? Kate and April are forced to face up to events from their younger years, their mother's desertion, and their long-deteriorating relationship with one another. Some lives will be lost and others changed forever when the sisters' lives intersect. Will they be consumed by the wreckage, or will they be able to pick themselves up and take flight?

Reflected Passion—Erica Lawson   Where passion, reality, and destiny combine.
Dale Wincott is a 27-year-old woman born into Bostonian wealth and groomed to marry into the social hierarchy. Her mother is a hard-hearted society matriarch, but her father feels for his daughter and helps Dale find a life on her own as a furniture restorer. Françoise Marie Aurélie de Villerey is a 28-year-old Countess, born into the French aristocracy and forced to marry a count much older than herself. For ten years, she was his trophy wife, forced to endure his perverted desires, until the day he finally died. He had broken her emotionally and she no longer cared for what life had to offer, slipping from one sexual partner to another as often as she changed her clothes. Until... that one night when Françoise looked up during a sexual encounter and saw Dale watching her from the mirror. A veritable angel, full of innocence and curiosity, who touched her very soul. Through the mirror, Françoise embraces life anew, while for Dale it is a powerful awakening, forcing her to discover not only her sensual nature, but the inner strength she possesses.

The One—JM Dragon Phil (Philomena) Casters loves her work as a pilot, above everything else in her life except Ming, her married lover. Phil needs to enhance her status in the community before asking Ming to leave behind her wealthy husband. Rosa Moran a teacher, raised by missionaries in China after the death of her parents. She loves the country of her birth and the people. Her English grandfather desperately wants her to live with him to atone for the guilt he feels about the death of her parents. He sends her a letter requesting her to come home. When Phil flies to the mission to deliver the letter to Rosa, neither can envisage the chain of events about to take place. It starts as a collaboration to save four children, leading them to the surreal private paradise of Langshow. Could this be the perfect place for the children and Rosa to settle? Phil is not so sure. Chang, an old friend from Rosa's childhood lives in Langshow and makes no bones about the fact that he wants Rosa. All thoughts of Ming disappear as Phil tries to fight her attraction to Rosa. However there is the little matter of an innocent misunderstanding—Rosa thinks Phil is a man. *The One* is a romance with everything, love, intrigue, misunderstandings with a happy conclusion—the only question—who gets the girl?

The Chronicles of Ratha: Book 2 A Lion Among the Lambs—Erica Lawson   It has been three years since Jordana Laren's path first crossed the Noorthi's - three years since she's had a drink, had sex and a life of her own. Her only excitement has been spent keeping up with her two year-old daughter, Rice, who is definitely a chip off the old block. All has been peaceful until one of the colonists becomes sick. Bad news shifts to worse news when the disease spreads through their community. Unable to get proper medicine, Jordana is forced to rely on the Noorthi healers to come up with a cure. Soon the herbs run out, leaving her with no choice but to search for more on the Noorthi home planet. What is supposed to be a simple pickup flight turns into a nightmare. Can Jordana believe in herself like her Noorthi sisters do? Only then can she fulfill her destiny as The Chosen One. Follow the colorful cast of characters in this action-packed adventure sequel as they traverse the galaxy. Of course, nothing ever goes smoothly when Jordana is involved.

Cowgirl Up—Ali Spooner When the new ranch hand, Coal Bryan, arrives at the MC2, the last thing she's looking for is love. Her co-workers are surprised when Coal turns out to be female. Coal, used to the reaction, quickly earns the respect of the crew with her work ethic and skill with horses. Coal uses the strenuous work and friendship of the ranch hands to try and forget her broken past. Melissa Conway, owner of MC2, offers Coal a place to live in her home. They both are shocked to find they are linked in a way neither of them imagined. Mary Leah, Melissa's sister, arrives at the ranch to recover from a recent tragedy. The attraction between Mary Leah and Coal is instant and mutual. Can the three women survive their personal dilemmas? The love and friendship they develop certainly helps but will it be enough to bring them together. Ride along with the MC2, for boot scootin', butt kickin', dirt eatin', rodeo adventures, with a love story thrown into the mix.

If I Were a Boy—Erin O'Reilly Katie McGuire appears to have it all. A devoted husband, a job she loved, and a comfortable lifestyle. Helen Swenson is a successful financial director of a prominent investment firm, with an unfaithful husband, and few friends. Their husbands' annual trip to Padre Island National Seashore to reunite with their air force pilot squad becomes a pivotal point for the two women. Their lives take on a completely new meaning when an undeniable magnetism between them draws them together. Passion and secrecy becomes the norm, as they have no choice but to succumb to their attraction. Can the vacation love affair continue? When they leave for their respective homes, will they regret what happened? Life is not that easy to change and the people around them are the hardest to convince. There is no more powerful motivation than love. Except hate and there are plenty of people who want to see their relationship destroyed. Will Katie and Helen be able to make a life together work or succumb to doubts and the pressures of family? This story will fill you with the thrill of passion and the tenderness of love.

The Chronicles of Ratha: Book 1 Children of the Noorthi—Erica Lawson Jordana Laren is a hard-drinking, hard-fighting womanizer, who works as a freighter pilot in her spare time. Her latest customer drugs her, steals her ship, and abandons her on a desert hellhole called Rigeus, infamous penal planet for the worst women criminals. Her chances of survival aren't looking good. She has no food, water, or weapons, and the nearest bar is a million miles away. Just when she's ready to write her last will and testament, Jordana is rescued by a group of barely-clad women. Has she found nirvana? Her own personal harem seems like a possibility, until the intercession of their enemy, the Velkren. Their leader, Vel, remembers Jordana well, and not fondly. But why is Vel on this planet, surrounded by murderers, thieves, and bad-tempered bitches? Jordana knows Vel isn't a prisoner, so why is her nemesis on Rigeus mining mud, of all things? Jordana knows only one thing. She has to get off the planet before Vel kills her. Unfortunately, the women who saved her reveal themselves to be holy. They are the Noorthi, and Jordana's dream of endless debauchery becomes a nightmare of eternal servitude. The Noorthi make her one of them, marking her with a wrist tattoo, and leaving her no choice but to protect them with her life. The last thing Jordana wants is to become involved in galactic politics or heroic actions. But the tattoo ochre in her body is suddenly giving her morals and scruples, not to mention a better vocabulary! And she really can't pass up a chance to outwit Vel, whose megalomaniac plans are endangering not only the Noorthi, but the civilized galaxy itself. But Jordana is torn. Does she stop Vel at all costs, or does she get out from under the thumb of the Noorthi while she can? Some things were never meant to be easy…

Nesting—Renee MacKenzie Macy Stokes, a divorced mother who is struggling with her sexual identity, jumps at a once-in-a-lifetime opportunity to help her friends. She doesn't foresee it will put her in jeopardy of losing her son, Jeremiah. Fresh out of high school, Cam Webber travels to Augusta, Georgia, to reconcile with her aunt. When she learns that's impossible, she determines to gain acceptance from her aunt's partner, Sharon. Meanwhile, Cam sets her sights on Macy, but Macy has other ideas. Kenny Brewer is a good old boy who loves his wife, Dorianne, even when he thinks she's gone totally off her rocker. Dorianne gets it in her head that a local woman is her long-lost half-sister. But soon, her obsession with that is eclipsed by medical problems that involve them all. Set in Augusta, Georgia, *Nesting* explores the age-old issues of guilt, regret, and redemption, and the part they play in driving people to create and protect family-at any cost.

E-Books, Print, Free e-books

Visit our website for more publications available online.

www.affinityebooks.com

Published by Affinity E-Book Press NZ LTD
Canterbury, New Zealand

Registered Company 2517228

Printed in Great Britain
by Amazon